The Tiger and the Coronet

A Hammond & Circle Mystery

AG Barnett

Oddmoor Press

Copyright © 2025 by A.G. Barnett

All rights reserved.

No part of this book may be reproduced in any form or by any electronic or mechanical means, including information storage and retrieval systems, without written permission from the author, except for the use of brief quotations in a book review.

Prologue

The tiger opened one eye in response to the noise of human laughter. Its keen eyesight scanned the darkness in front of its cage until it met a light bobbing across the lawn from the main house, prompting its second eye to open. Soft, murmuring voices reached its ears before a shriek of laughter again pierced the silence.

Two humans came into view from the darkness and the enormous cat raised its head in curiosity. Was this perhaps an unexpected mealtime? She was hungry. She was always hungry.

As they came closer to the cage, locked arm in arm, both grinning and giggling, the tiger realised this would not be another mealtime. They carried no food, only something shining dully in the dim light behind their torchlight.

One of them stepped forward, moving closer to the steel bars that permanently veiled the tigers' view of the world. One figure threw the dully gleaming object through the bars and it made a sharp clang as it hit the concrete floor of the enclosure and rolled in a wide curve before stopping, upright, against the rear wall.

The figures retreated into the night and the tiger laid its head down once more.

Chapter One

Flo knocked using the brass knocker on the bright red door. After a few moments, a middle-aged, plump woman in a somber black dress which seemed to match the tone of her expression opened it.

"Yes?" she said in a tone that suggested that answering the door was a major inconvenience to her.

"Is this Jessie Circle's residence?" Flo asked, fearing she had arrived at the wrong address.

"Residence might be stretching the term," the woman said with a sigh as she moved aside and gestured for Flo to enter. "It's one more of her stops along the way to ruin."

Flo gave a small smile as she entered, unsure how to take the woman's tone.

Flo surveyed the hallway into which she had been led. The house being newly rented and unfamiliar to her. It was a modest place and didn't feel truly lived in. There had been two other places Jessie had called 'home' in the few months Flo had known her. Both had felt the same. Temporary.

"Ah, here she is," the woman muttered.

"Flo!' Jessie cried as she appeared at the top of the stairs. She was still pulling on a pair of trousers, wearing only a bra above. "I see you've met Hardcastle. Isn't she a treasure?"

"By calling me a treasure, she means she dug me up somewhere," muttered the woman in black.

"Um, yes," Flo said, finding herself, as she so often did around Jessie Circle, as though she were a leaf caught in a powerful gust of wind.

"One minute," Jessie said, raising a finger at Flo before vanishing again.

As the silence between Flo and the woman she now knew as Hardcastle grew, she felt the need to fill it.

"I'm afraid I must be early," she said.

"Oh, I doubt it," Hardcastle replied. "I'd wager that one hasn't been on time for anything in her life."

"Right," Jessie said, appearing at the top of the stairs again, now fully dressed. She dashed down and kissed Flo on both cheeks before turning to Hardcastle.

"Would you mind terrible taking care of the thing upstairs?"

Hardcastle rolled her eyes and tutted, but didn't say no.

"Shall we?" Jessie said, turning back to Flo with a gesture towards the door.

"Where are you going?" A male voice came from above.

Flo turned to see a young man who looked as though he had been chiseled from marble. He wore only a pair of white undershorts, and from his rustled hair and the way he rubbed at one eye, it was clear he had just woken.

"Got to go away for a couple of days, James," Jessie said lightly. "Hardcastle here will make sure you get breakfast before you go on your way."

"My name's John," the man replied in confusion.

"Good for you!" Jessie cried, and with one last wave, she opened the front door and was gone.

"The road to ruin," Hardcastle muttered as Flo followed her out.

"Who was that?!" Flo asked in a shocked whisper as she met Jessie on the street.

"John," Jessie shrugged as she waved down a black cab, "didn't you just hear him say so? Anyway, there will be plenty of time to catch up on the train."

"The train? Where are we going?"

"Wales!" Jessie said excitedly. "We're going to help with a problem of national significance."

"National significance?" Flo said, feeling a rising dread. "Oh dear lord, what have you got us involved in now?!"

"I have absolutely no idea," Jessie said as she opened the door of the car that had stopped in front of them, "Isn't it marvellous?!"

Chapter Two

"That's all the information you have?" Flo asked.

"Afraid so," Jessie answered lightly.

After a short cab drive they had dashed through paddington station, pausing only to buy a ticket, and board a train heading west. Once aboard, Flo had continued to attempt to discover their destination and the reason for heading to it.

Jessie had received a telegram from a man called Hugo Rathbone, who apparently was a viscount residing in a seventeenth century pile in Monmouthshire, Wales. According to Jessie, it had contained a request for their help to solve a mystery that was a matter of national importance.

Flo had to take Jessie's word for it that there was no more information, as she had apparently thrown the telegram on the fire after reading it. Jessie claimed she did this for security reasons. Though, as Flo had pointed out, if the telegram didn't actually reveal any more information than this, it was hardly a national security risk. Jessie had simply said that maybe Flo wasn't cut out for such an important mission.

"I'm sure I've read of Viscount Rathbone before," Flo said.

"I'm not surprised. Hardcastle says he's quite an influential chap, though a bit eccentric."

"That's another thing. Who on earth is this Hardcastle?"

"She," Jessie said dramatically, "is an angel sent from heaven." She paused and frowned. "Or a devil sent from hell, I haven't quite decided yet. In any case, she's the only housekeeper I've had that has lasted more than a month and she seems to know everything about everything. Which is good enough for me."

"And is the young man who was at the top of the stairs one of the reasons you get through so many housekeepers?" Flo asked with a raised eyebrow.

"Oh no, I think the prospect of finding a half dressed man walking about the house occasionally is the only reason some of them stayed as long as they did."

Flo burst out laughing before trying to stifle her fit of giggles in the face of some stern looks from fellow passengers in their carriage.

She turned to look at the English countryside as it sped past the window. The fields were a lighter green than normal, having been scorched by the unusually hot and dry weather over the last few weeks.

When she looked back at Jessie, she saw she was staring down at a newspaper on her lap and filling in the crossword there.

She was sitting on a train to Wales, with no clue whatsoever why, and rather than being scared or worried, she only felt exhilaration and excitement. This, she thought, was the effect on her life of Jessie Circle.

Chapter Three

At Newport station, a blank-faced man in a chauffeur's uniform greeted them and then led them to an Austin Twenty that rumbled and waddled them along like a tugboat through a choppy sea.

After only a short drive, they turned left into a driveway that ran alongside a lake and had their first sight of Trelawny House.

A large, square building, set amongst trees in green parkland. It had a rather overly grand covered entrance made up of a series of arches around the three sides that extended out from the house.

"What on earth is that?!" Jessie exclaimed.

Flo turned to see her staring out of the window at a man who was squaring up to the most extraordinary animal Flo had ever seen.

"He's boxing with it!" Flo said, hardly able to believe her own eyes.

"Driver," Jessie demanded, "What on earth is that animal?"

"It's a kangaroo, Miss," the driver replied. "Mr Rathbone has rather an interesting collection of exotic animals in his menagerie."

Of course, Flo had seen pictures of the creatures before. She just hadn't expected it to be so large, so humanlike as it stood on its hind legs, throwing jabs with its forearms at the man in front of it.

"Bonko is a boxing kangaroo," the driver said. As if this made complete sense to him and would surely do so to Flo and Jessie.

Before Flo could ask further questions, the bizarre scene had disappeared from view behind a row of trees as they pulled up in a wide turning circle in front of the house. As two young boys dealt with their luggage, they were greeted between the arches of the entrance by a tall, rangy man with a large, beaked nose. His rather birdlike appearance was enhanced by the fact he had an enormous parrot on his right shoulder.

"Good morning!" He said cheerily with a wide grin before shaking their hands enthusiastically. "Hugo Rathbone, so good of you to come."

Before either of them could make their own introductions, the parrot let out a stream of obscenities that had Flo feeling her cheeks flush. There was a moment of silence as Hugo Rathbone's eyes darted between them, when Jessie burst out laughing and Flo found herself following in suit.

"This is Blue Boy," Hugo laughed. "his name rather chose itself, as you can see."

After introducing themselves, they placed Blue Boy in a huge cage in the main hall and then took the others into a drawing-room. The room had a sort of old world opulence, like the rest of the house. The smell of polished wood mixed with the scent of flowers which were dotted around in vases, and soft leather sofas and armchairs sat invitingly around a table where tea, muffins and cakes were delivered on silver trays by a swift-footed maid.

"Thank you for coming so quickly," Hugo said, seeming serious for the first time since they had arrived. "I'm afraid I've got myself into a bit of a sticky situation and time is short to resolve it."

"What exactly has happened?" Flo asked.

Hugo placed his teacup on the table and leaned forward, hands clasped together as though praying. "Have you heard of the Coronet of George?"

"You mean King George?" Flo asked, her pulse quickening, not just at this potential link with British royalty, but also at a sense that she knew something of what was about to come.

"Yes. Well, sort of," Huge said awkwardly. He steepled his long fingers in front of him and took a deep breath. "The coronet was made for George, who was prince of Wales then, to wear at King Edward's coronation. Of course, after the death of Edward, George became king, and they made a new coronet for the new prince of Wales, Edward."

"As fascinating as I find your quaint British customs, what does this coronet have to do with your problem?"

Flo realised she was open-mouthed and closed her lips before anyone noticed. The first thing to have shocked her was that Viscount Trelawny could bandy about names of the royals as though they were simply members of his local gentleman's club. Jessie, referring to the monarchy as a 'quaint British custom', had tipped her over the edge.

Hugo thought, just smiled. "Well, it's all rather embarrassing, really." He began. "Now that the coronet isn't the current one, it's rather of an oddity in the crown jewel stakes. It's been decided that it will be gifted to the people

The Tiger and the Coronet

of Wales in order to further cement ties between the two great nations."

He had said this last piece as though repeating it, and by his rather sarcastic tone, he thought it nonsense.

"Until now, the coronet has been under my security, a temporary measure until something could be done with it."

"The repatriation," Flo said, with a sudden realisation.

Hugo nodded, his beak-like nose bobbing up and down like a bird taking water. "I'm sure you've read about it."

"For those of us less up to date on current affairs," Jessie said, "a quick recap?"

"As the coronet is no longer part of the official British Crown Jewels," Hugo continued, "it is being repatriated to the people of Wales to strengthen the bond between nations."

Jessie looked at Flo quizzically.

"It's a political thing," Flo said with a wave of her hand.

"Last year, Parliament disestablished the Church of England in Wales," Hugo said, "with the mounting troubles in Ireland, there's a feeling that something should be done to show unity."

"If I remember correctly, the King is presenting the coronet to Welsh dignitaries?" Flo said.

Hugo sighed and leaned back in his chair, somewhat deflated. "Yes, in three days at a ceremony at Cardiff Castle. There's just one issue."

"Which is?" Jessie asked.

"I seem to have mislaid the coronet."

There was a silence where Hugo studied his hands, and Jessie and Flo exchanged glances.

"Mislaid?" Flo repeated slowly.

"I know," Hugo said with a sheepish grin, "it does sound somewhat silly, doesn't it? The thing is, it was here last night. We all saw it! No one's left the house, staff or guests, and there's no sign of a break in. The only people to come since Wednesday are you two kind souls rushing to my aid."

"What were your security arrangements? Surely you didn't just leave the thing lying around?" Jessie asked, making Flo wince at her forthrightness.

"Oh no, I had a special safe made to the highest standards. It was going to be by my bedside, but when it arrived, I'm afraid it was too heavy to get up the stairs. So it's in The Gilt room. I can show you if you like?"

"As good a place to start as any," Jessie said, clapping her hands together and rising.

Flo waited until Hugo had moved ahead of them towards the door before pulling Jessie to a halt by her elbow.

"Jessie," she hissed, we can't possibly get involved in this!"

Hugo paused and looked back at them.

"Could you give us a moment?" Jessie said with a smile.

"Of course, Hugo smiled. I'll wait outside."

He left the room and Jessie turned to Flo with arms folded. "What's the matter?"

"What's the matter?! What's the matter is that a priceless part of the Crown Jewels is expected to be in the King's own hands in two days! This man, who keeps a parrot that swears like a sailor and a boxing kangaroo, mind you, is expecting us to save the day!"

"Damn exciting, isn't it?" Jessie smiled.

"No! Its lunacy is what it is. We're not detectives Jessie, we can't be relied upon to sort this out in time!"

"Oh, come on Flo. We can at least try."

"He needs to bring the proper authorities in," Flo protested. "The police, government officials, MI5."

"Let's just hear him out and have a look at the safe, shall we?" Jessie said in a voice that was clearly intended to be soothing, but was rather spoilt by the grin of excitement she wore as she turned to the door.

Flo sighed and followed her back out into the hallway, where the parrot Blue Boy immediately launched into another filthy tirade of swearwords.

Chapter Four

The Gilt room lay at the end of a long passageway, with only one door as access. The room lived up to its name.

The room's wood panelled walls were almost entirely covered in gold leaf, save for central panels where scenes including bare-chested mythological figures were painted directly onto the wood.

"Oh, yes" Hugo said, turning and noting their open-mouthed reaction to the room, "it is quite something, isn't it?"

"It's magnificent," Flo said breathlessly as she moved to the fireplace surround her hadn't reaching out to two golden lions at its heart.

"The safe's here," Hugo said, gesturing to the corner of the room where a large iron safe sat like a grotesque monster in this room of finery.

They both stepped over to it and crouched down to look inside the already open door.

"Do you use the safe for anything else?" Jessie asked.

"Oh no, I have a personal one for odd bits and bobs, but this was just for the coronet."

"And how many keys are there?" Flo asked, straightening up as Jessie continued to peer at the lock and run her hand around the rough metal of the safe's surface.

"Oh, um. Three, I think. I lost one some time ago, and I've got one here that was in my bedside drawer and the third one's in the drawer here," he said, moving to a small sideboard with ornately carved, thin legs. He pulled one of the two drawers open and held up a key.

"And where is that one normally kept?" Flo asked.

Hugo gave a nervous chuckle and moved to the door, closing it gently. "Better to be completely honest in this sort of situation, don't you think?" He said, his long, slender hands wringing in front of him as he looked at them both sheepishly. "The thing is, I haven't been awfully strict on security, never needed to."

"In general," Jessie said with a grin, "it's better to implement good security before you are robbed, rather than after."

Flo tensed again at the careless way Jessie addressed a viscount, but Hugo just laughed, his head jerking back as he guffawed.

"Quite right!" He exclaimed. "Lesson learned there, I suppose. The truth is, I normally just left the key in the door of the safe." He looked at both their slightly incredulous expressions, "The house is locked up every night of course," he added weakly.

"That explains why the safe doesn't look to have been tampered with," Jessie said, frowning down at the iron cube.

"Has anything else been taken or disturbed?" Flo asked, "Locks tampered with, windows broken, that sort of thing?"

"No, nothing. I had my housemaid Miss Evans get the staff to check everything this morning, the butler's come down with a touch of flu, and there was no sign of anything unusual." He shrugged.

"You mentioned guests earlier?" Flo said.

"Yes," Hugo nodded, "got quite a number here at the moment. I'm certain none of them are nothing to do with this business, but I asked them all to stay in any case."

"I think that's probably for the best," Jessie nodded, "and none of them have left the house at all since the coronet went missing?"

"No, none." Hugo replied. "I decided to send for you immediately, but had to tell them about the coronet obviously. Had to give them a reason they were now prisoners here."

"Why exactly did you send for us?" Flo asked, glancing at Jessie. "Why not call the police?"

"My dear Miss Hammond," Hugo said, his eyes widening, "you must understand how delicate this situation is. In just two days, the King will be expecting to hold that coronet in his very hands! If word got out, there would be an absolute scandal. I wouldn't be able to show myself anywhere in England!"

"I'm not sure the situation will be any better if he arrives to find you have put the matter in the hands of two amateurs who failed to find the thing," Flo snapped back.

There was an awkward pause in which Flo's cheeks slowly turned ever more crimson.

"I'm sorry," she said as her mind raced through the possibility that speaking to a lord of the realm in that way might actually be treasonous.

Suddenly, Rathbone's head jerked backwards as he roared into a laugh where he was soon joined by Jessie's unfeasibly loud hawing. Flo couldn't help but begin to smile, and then laugh, herself.

"You're quite right, of course," Rathbone said once the three of them have laughed themselves out. "But I'm afraid I've never been known for making the best decisions, so I freely admit that this might be another stinker, but I'm afraid I don't really know what else to do. Like I said, I really can't afford to let the authorities know this has happened on my watch. Besides," he said, spreading his long thin fingers in front of him, "I can't see how the blasted thing has left the house. No one's left!"

"How many people are staying here currently?" Jessie asked.

"We have six house guests, as well as staff, of course. I'm afraid I don't know the exact number."

Flo felt her eyebrows rise automatically. Someone who didn't even know how many staff they employ was certainly of a level of wealth she had not encountered before.

"And are they friends, family?" Jessie continued.

"Oh, friends, acquaintances, I like to keep something of an open house for guests. It makes life interesting, don't you think?" he said with a warm smile.

"Well, I think the current situation would definitely class as interesting," Jessie said, causing Rathbone's smile to falter slightly.

"Can you tell us about your guests?" Flo asked.

"Oh, right." Rathbone said, leaning forward. "There's Charles Becker and Elizabeth Armstrong,"

"Oh!" Flo said, before she could stop herself.

"You know them?" Rathbone asked.

"Oh, no," Flo answered, feeling her cheeks flush, "I just know them from the papers."

"Ah, of course," Rathbone laughed. "The papers do

seem to enjoy lurid tales of the 'Bright Young Things', as they're known. The gang's always gallivanting around London, causing mischief from what I've heard. Not had the chance to come along to one of their bash's yet myself."

"I have," Jessie said with a smile, "and I think I remember Charles Becker, actually. Very much one of the leading lights as I remember it."

Rathbone gave a small chuckle. "That's Charles, always ready with a joke and a drink."

"And the others staying?" Flo asked.

"There's Mary Preston," Rathbone continued. "She's from an old family, friends of ours going back generations, up in Yorkshire. She's got some aspirations to be a film actress, which is causing her family all sorts of panic," he laughed.

"Then there's Ruth Robbins and Thadd Barnes."

"Thadd?" Jessie said curiously. "That's an unusual name."

Hugo raised an eyebrow. "Says a woman named Circle?"

"Touche," Jessie said with a smile.

"It's short for Thaddeus. They're both local dignitaries of sorts, here for the ceremony. Ruth is the adopted daughter of old David Robbin's. Major landowner out Swansea way, but he's been taken ill so she's here in his stead. Thadd is from the Welsh Ministry of Agriculture and Fisheries."

"The Welsh ministry?" Flo said in surprise.

Rathbone smiled. "Came into effect last year. No idea what they do, but it's the cause of much pride around these parts, as I'm sure Thadd will tell you."

"And the sixth guest?" Flo asked.

Hugo frowned for a moment, before his face cleared in

realisation, "Oh, Robert! Of course, Robert Pearce. I don't know him too well, truth be told. Quiet chap, bookish sort. Came into money from some uncle or other and I rather fancy he's trying to 'fit in' with his new status."

"Did any of them invite themselves over?" Jessie asked, "Maybe this had been planned for some time?"

"Oh, I think pretty much all of them did," Hugo answered. "Trelawny has become a bit of a drop in, drop out kind of place. It's how I like it. Lots of faces, new and old, and lots of entertainment."

Flo nodded thoughtfully, wondering if Rathbone's form of entertainment would stretch to faking a theft of national significance.

A gilded clock which sat on the mantlepiece began to announce the hour with a melodic pattern of chimes.

"Ah," Rathbones said, slapping his hands on his knees. "If the rest of the staff have managed to sort themselves out, we should be due for cocktails on the terrace. You can meet the other guests there and begin your sleuthing." He stood up and brushed down his trousers. "As I said, Jenkins, my butler, is out of action at the moment. That's why I came to meet you myself when I saw you from the window. Only staff left seem to be a lot of dizzy maids and Evans, the housekeeper which is a bit of a strain. I dare not let Jenkins get word that anything's the matter though, the mans so dedicated he'd be up and about no matter how ill he is."

"We saw someone on the way in," Flo said, rising from her seat as well. "He seemed to be fighting a kangaroo."

Hugo gave a short bark of laughter. "Oh yes, that would be Hector and Bonko. Got a surprisingly good jab."

Flo and Jessie exchanged curious glances as they followed him out of the room, unsure if he had been complementing the staff member or the kangaroo.

Chapter Five

They stepped through a set of French doors which led out onto a wide terrace overlooking the south facing lawns some ten feet below which stretched out in front of them until it reached the tree line of a small wood.

The house guests were already gathered around a drinks trolley that had been wheeled out for the occasion.

"Do you know what?" Jessie said loudly, before Rathbone could introduce them. "I could absolutely murder a drink."

The group around the trolley turned as one to look at them.

"Look out, everyone," said a young man with a flop of dark hair and a smile that could only be described as being on the mischievous side of decent. "We've got an American in our midst and we know how starved of the good stuff they've been."

A ripple of laughter ran through the small crowd as Jessie moved towards him.

"Charles Becker," she said with an outstretched hand,

"Jessie Circle. We met at a party in London earlier this year."

"Of course," he said with a smile as he took her hand. "Absolutely delighted."

"So you're here to find Hugo's missing crown," said a pretty, round-faced brunette next to him as she extended her hand, "I'm Beth."

Jessie took her hand as Flo shook Charles's, following along behind her.

"It's a coronet, Beth, not a crown," Hugo said as he moved to the drinks trolley and began preparing a fresh batch of cocktails.

"Is there a difference?" Beth asked with a light laugh.

"Crowns are for kings and queens," said Rathbone, "coronets are for princes and below."

"I just can't get enough of your funny English customs," Jessie smiled as she moved along the group to a woman with a messy blonde bob and round, watery eyes.

"Ruth Robbins," the woman said in a soft Welsh accent as they shook hands, "I've always wanted to visit America."

"Well, I'm sure you'd be welcomed as long as you have money in your pocket," Jessie answered with wry smile.

"Let me extend a very warm welcome to our fine country," said a young man moving from the back of the group, pushing aside a short, tubby man in glasses as he did so. "I'm Thaddeus Barnes, but call me Thadd. I represent the country of Wales here this weekend, and the Welsh Ministry of Agriculture and Fisheries specifically."

"Then I shall make sure I'm on my best behaviour," Jessie her face suddenly serious, causing Charles to snort with laughter and Flo to redden as she continued to shake hands in the wake of Jessie.

"And you are?" she said, peering round at the man Thaddeus had blocked.

"Robert Pearce," he answered in a thin, high voice.

"My name is Mary Preston," the woman next to him said in a lofty tone, cutting in abruptly before pulling on a cigarette from the long black holder in her hand.

"Wonderful to meet you," Jessie smiled. "All of you," she said, turning to them all.

Flo watched her friend with interest and envy, in awe of how at ease she always seemed to be in any situation. Flo had spent much of her life feeling on the outside of things. Her three older brothers had been the focus of her parents. They were loving and kind to her, but never attentive. She was always somewhere in the background, occasionally emerging into the light, but very much a bit-part player. She realised with a jolt that she had allowed this to continue into her adulthood. Jessie, though, Jessie seemed unencumbered by anything.

"Well, cheers to meetings!" Charles said, snapping Flo out of her revery and draining the last of his glass.

"I realise you're all having a jolly pleasant time and all," Rathbone said, handing cocktails to both Flo and Jessie, "but this is a serious business. I must have that blasted coronet back by Monday or there will be hell to pay."

"But Hugo, my dear man," Charles said, "that's why these wonderful ladies have joined us. The super sleuths who cracked that case in the Cotswolds. We all saw it in the paper."

"Things often sound more dramatic in the papers," Flo said, feeling somewhat awkward at the praise.

Charles raised a sardonic eyebrow. "That's quite a statement from the woman who wrote the piece."

Flo forced a smile onto her face, "I'm afraid the editors

like to take a little artistic license to make the thing more sensational when a murder is involved."

"This little missing coronet must seem of no great importance to you after such a case," Elizabeth said, clearly amused.

"It's not about how important the crime is," Jessie said with a smile that didn't reach her eyes. "It's about intriguing it is, don't you think?"

Elizabeth seemed unsure how to respond to this and glanced towards Charles.

"Why don't we forget about the coronet for now," Jessie continued, "and enjoy ourselves. I'm in no doubt we'll find the coronet and I can only hope that it's all an innocent misunderstanding."

There was a pause as the group seemed to mull over these words. Flo's gaze moved around the gathered faces and found herself mentally assessing each of them as she did so.

Charles Becker seemed to be a cocky and somewhat arrogant young man who seemed to have a perpetual sneering smile, which made her want to slap him.

Elizabeth Armstrong, or Beth as she had introduced herself, was clearly besotted with Charles, whether or not she knew it. The way she looked at him left Flo in no doubt of that. Flo had initially thought her a silly young woman, but there was something else there that was more unpleasant. A nastiness that floated just beneath the surface.

Ruth Robbins was what Flo's grandmother could have called a 'wet lettuce'. She had soulful eyes with a dreamy expression that seemed to match the white linen dress she wore under a rainbow striped knitted cardigan.

Robert Pearce was a thick-spectacled, owlish sort of man who looked as though he wasn't sure he should be there. She suspected that he gave that impression wherever he was.

Mary was tall, elegant and beautiful, but in a vaguely unreal way. As though she were a porcelain doll brought to life with an attitude just as cold as her metaphorical skin.

Thaddeus Barnes seemed to Flo to be rather young to be a representative of a governmental body, but then she supposed the welsh office of the ministry of agriculture and fisheries was relatively young itself, bearing in mind she had never heard of it.

A strange collection of people all in all. Whether any of them would have the desire or gumption to steal the coronet, she did not know. Having now met the rather eccentric Hugo Rathbone, she was quickly coming to the conclusion that the coronet had merely been mislaid somewhere. First thing in the morning, she resolved to conduct a thorough search of the house, where she was sure she'd find this important piece of British history down the back of a sofa or being sat on by the parrot.

"Miss Hammond," Thaddeus said to her, pulling her from her contemplation. "I wonder if I could have a word with you?" he gestured with his arm, suggesting that this was a conversation he wanted to have in private.

She moved with him across the terrace until he paused a distance that would mean they were not overheard.

"As I'm sure you know, I represent the Welsh authorities here," he said rather grandly.

"Hugo told me you worked at the new ministry of agriculture and fisheries," Flo replied.

Thaddeus raised his chin slightly, "I assure you that this is only the first step in Wales, becoming more autonomous. It is quite the honour to be in my post at such a historic time."

"Oh, I'm sure," Flo said, hoping she sounded more sincere than she felt about such a statement. "What was it you wanted to talk to me about?"

"Oh, right," he said, his eyes darting to the rest of the gathering where Jessie's raucous laugh was galloping across the terrace like a herd of rhino. "The thing is, I know you're a journalist."

Flo felt herself wince slightly. She still wasn't entirely comfortable with what had happened to her career over the last few months.

Yes, she had had her first proper journalistic article published, and even under her own name. Somehow, Jessie had had a hand in that, but she was unclear how.

"It's imperative," Thaddeus continued, "That this is handled the correct way in the press."

"Oh," Flo said, "I'm sure there won't be much of a story here. The coronet is bound to turn up."

"Of course, of course," he answered quickly, shaking his head dismissively as he looked over her shoulder at where the others were talking.

Was he worried about someone overhearing them?

"Whether or not it turns up again, it's important the incident is painted in the correct light, you see."

"I'm not sure I do see Mr Barnes?"

"Call me Thadd, please," he said dismissively before leaning in even closer to her. "I'm sure you're aware of what an important time this is for Wales. There is talk of a truce being declared in Ireland, and it could change everything. There has never been a better time for the Welsh people to assert its right to self-govern."

"I did not know there was such a desire for more independence," Flo said, "but I'm not sure what this has to do with me?"

He gave a barely disguised sigh of impatience before continuing, "An incident like this could be very useful to our cause. Hugo's a good man, but he's hardly the type that should be put in charge of something like this. It could go towards us making our case that, politically, England shows a disregard for the Welsh people."

"I'm sorry," Flo said, "but I'm really not a political journalist at all, and I certainly wouldn't want to get involved in anything like you're suggesting."

"He's not trying to convert you to his cause, is he?" A soft voice said from behind Flo. She turned to see the large, watery blue eyes of Ruth Robbins as she drifted closer.

"We were having a private conversation," Thadd said in clipped tones.

"I'm afraid he has a rather old-fashioned vision of what Wales should be," With continued in her distracted, dreamy voice. "I must say, it's wonderful to have you here."

"Thank you," Flo said

Flo glanced over at Jessie, who was holding Hugo Rathbone, Charles Becker and Elizabeth Armstrong in rapt attention as she recounted some tale or other. Flo dreaded to think what the content might be.

"When Ruth says 'old fashioned'," Thadd continued, "what she really means is progressive in a practical way. A way that brings our great nation to the top table where we can make a difference to people's lives."

"Like England's little pet dragon," Ruth said, one side of her mouth rising in amusement.

Thadd huffed, but was prevented from answering by a shout of welcome from Hugo Rathbone. All eyes turned towards the wide, shallow steps that led down from the terrace onto the sweeping gardens.

The Tiger and the Coronet

The man who lightly jogged up the steps was clearly the figure Flo had seen at a distance boxing with a kangaroo, as they had arrived. He wore a loose white shirt which served to highlight his swarthy complexion. His long dark hair fell down to his shoulders, one thick lock hanging over his forehead.

His deep, brown eyes shone as he turned them towards Flo as he passed her small group and her heart fluttered slightly in her chest.

"Everyone!" Rathbone said, meeting the man in the middle of the terrace and clasping one arm around his shoulders. "This is Hector. He manages my little menagerie here." He guided Hector back to where he had been standing with Jessie and began introductions.

"Try not to go too weak at the knees," Ruth said quietly in Flo's ear.

Flo felt her cheeks redden as she turned to the young woman, who wore an amused smile on her face.

"Oh, don't worry, everyone here lusts after Hector," she said casually.

"Really, Ruth!" Thadd hissed at her, "Could you please show some decorum?"

"And I really must introduce you to her partner in crime, so to speak." Their host said as he guided Hector and Jessie towards Flo.

Jessie waggled her eyebrows theatrically at her before Flo quickly looked away from her to see the bemused face of the young man approaching.

"You are... criminals?" He said in a thick foreign accent, looking between Flo and Jessie.

"Oh!" Hugo cried in amusement, "Sorry, old boy, just a figure of speech. I forget sometimes that the Argentinians don't share our curious English expressions. These two ladies have come to find out what's happened to the coronet."

Hector's eyes narrowed. "I have told you, Mr Rathbone, that I did not take of it!"

"No, no, of course." Hugo said soothingly. "They just going to work out where it's got to, that's all. Not accuse anyone."

"Surely that's exactly what they're here to do?" Charles Becker said with a lopsided grin. "We're all suspects in the great robbery, eh?"

"It's simply too thrilling!" Elizabeth Armstrong giggled alongside him.

"I'm quite sure there's an innocent explanation," Thadd said, frowning at both of them.

"Spoken like a true thief in my view," Charles grinned back.

"How dare you!" Thadd snapped, his nostrils flaring in indignation. "I am a member of the Welsh ministry!"

"The ministry of fish Thadd, get some perspective." Charles laughed.

Thadd stepped towards him before pausing, shaking his head and turning away back towards the house.

"If you're quite all done causing these little dramatic scenes,' Rathbone said with one arched eyebrow, "then I suggest we head in for dinner before Evans bursts a blood vessel by trying to silently signal me."

He gestured to a woman with grey hair tied in a bun and a pug nose who stood near the French doors to the house with pursed lips and chin raised.

"She's a bit put out as I wouldn't let her answer the door to you," Rathbone said in a stage whisper to Flo as they headed past the red-cheeked housekeeper.

Chapter Six

As bowls of curried apricot and fresh mint soup were placed in front of the guests, it was mischievous and enthusiastic Charles Becker who started the small talk.

"Jessie, Flo, I assume you met Blue Boy when you arrived?"

"We did indeed," Jessie replied smiling "I haven't heard such language since the docks of New York."

There was a ripple of laughter before Rathbone spoke in between spoonfuls of soup.

"That bird is a better companion than most humans, believe me." He turned to Flo who was seated next to him. "He just has a powerful spirit and a colourful use of the English language." He winked before continuing. "It was Blue Boy that first piqued my interest in the animal kingdom. An old sailor in town passed away, and I bought his old cottage at auction to save it from falling into further disrepair."

Flo noticed Thadd look away sharply and Ruth smile at this, before Hugo continued.

"Old Blue Boy came with the place. Wouldn't do without him now, of course.Then, when I heard of a travelling zoo that was disbanding in the area, I started my little menagerie."

"How many animals do you have," Jessie asked.

"Oh, let's see now," Hugo said, placing his soup spoon down and reaching for his wine glass. "There's Blue Boy, of course. He's the only one that lives in the house. Then there's Bonko. He's the kangaroo I believe you saw as you arrived. Loves to box. There's Zeezee, he's a gibbon. Getting on a bit now, the poor chap. And finally, there's Duchess."

"A rather grand name," Jessie said, "and what is she?"

"A walking death trap," Charles chuckled.

"Duchess is perfectly safe," Hugo tutted at the young man. "Hector keeps her under lock and key, don't you, Hector?"

The Argentinian nodded, but his brow was creased and his expression hard.

Flo was surprised he was at dinner at all as a member of staff. He was clearly someone who had higher privileges than the rest of Trelawny's employees.

"Oh, I know, I know," Hugo said irritably, with a wave of his hand at Hector before turning to Flo again.

"Hector wants a larger enclosure for Duchess, and," he said, turning back to the young man opposite him, "I've said it will be done! I've already enquired in town at who might be available. Really, though, a few more weeks in her current home will do her no harm. Tigers are hardly the most delicate of creatures."

Flo choked slightly on her last mouthful of soup.

"You have a tiger?!"

Huge gave a wide grin, "she's an absolute beauty, isn't she that right Hector?"

"Yes, Mr Rathbone."

"I've told you, call me Hugo," the jovial host chided. "Tomorrow will give you a brief tour and you can meet my wild and wondrous pets."

"While you try to discover which of us stole the coronet," Charles Becker said with a laugh, which only Elizabeth joined in on.

There was a moment of silence as the gathering became momentarily engrossed in refilling their wine from the various decanters on the table.

"So," Charles continued, either unaware or despite the awkwardness his words had caused. "How do you plan on catching the thief?" He said, looking between Jessie and Flo.

"You seem very sure the coronet has been stolen," Jessie answered.

"Does anyone have a more reasonable explanation?" Charles said with an amused half smile.

"It could have been mislaid somehow."

Everyone turned to the doughy face of Robert Pearce, who had spoken and was blinking at them all through his thick spectacles.

"Mislaid?" Charles scoffed. "How on earth could it have been mislaid? The damned thing was in the safe."

Robert cleared his throat nervously before continuing in his high voice.

"If you remember, we had in fact had the coronet out after dinner last night. It could have been left somewhere where it fell down a gap or something."

"You tell him, Robert," Ruth Robbins said in her dreamy, amused voice. Causing him to flush a beetroot red.

"I'm afraid I find that rather unlikely," Mary Preston

said in her clipped, clear voice. "I saw Hugo returning it to The Gilt room as everyone retired for bed."

"Did you see him actually place the coronet in the safe?" Flo asked.

"No," Mary replied coldly, "But I watched him carry into the corridor. There's nowhere else it could have gone."

Flo felt the back of her neck prickly at the woman's tone.

"Well," she said flatly, "he could have remembered something he needed to do and turned back before reaching the room, putting down the coronet and forgetting where."

"I hardly think..." Mary began, but was cut off by Flo.

"Or, Hugo could have decided to steal the coronet himself, and merely wanted you as a convenient pair of eyes who would swear he had returned it to the safe. When, in fact, he had pocketed the piece to hide once everyone had gone to bed, to be retrieved at a later date."

Mary's eyes widened and turned to their host, snapping Flo back to reality and, in particular, the realisation she had just accused the viscount of theft. She turned to him, an apology already on her lips when the man in question gave what she was coming to realise was his normal reaction to most things. He laughed.

"Quite right!" He cried. "You see everyone? This is why I invited these two amazing women. They'll not beat about the bush and I daresay will clear this all up in no time. Good show." He shook his head in amusement as Mary Preston shot an annoyed glance at Flo.

"Hector," Jessie said in a tone loud enough to command the attention of the table. "Tell me, how did you come to be in South Wales instead of... Argentina was it?"

"Yes Miss," he answered as he finished filling up his glass with red wine for what, Flo was sure, was the third

The Tiger and the Coronet

time already." "I came with my father when I was young. We worked for Pablo Fistoria, a man from my country who ran the travelling zoo. I travelled and grew." He shrugged. "It was a good life."

"What happened to the zoo?" Flo asked.

"Sickness came, and many died." He passed and held Flo's gaze. "Pablo, and my father too. Then Mr Rathbone helped to save the animals."

"What else I could I do," Rathbone said, "the poor things were going to be put down! Then, of course, Hector here moved onto the estate to look after them all, as I have no experience of such things."

"And you added another pet to the menagerie…" Flo heard Mary Preston say quietly.

Rathbone cleared his throat as the housekeeper pushed a trolley through the door with the next course.

"Ah, the next course. Roasted grouse, I believe. As well as looking after the animals in my collection, Hector is also a fine shot when hunting. Isn't that right, Hector!" Hugo claimed, clapping his hands together.

"Yes, Mr Rathbone," Hector said with a nod and a flicker of a smile before the solemn expression he had worn since discussing his past had descended again.

Chapter Seven

Flo tugged at the hairbrush as it snagged on yet another knot in her hair.

"Come on, then, what are your impressions?" Jessie asked.

She was lounging in an armchair in the corner of her room, one leg slung over the arm as she sipped on a whisky and smoked a cigarette.

"My impression," Flo said, finally tugging the brush free, wincing in pain and dropping the thing on the dressing table with a sigh of defeat, "is that you've dragged us into a house full of strange, and not overly nice people, in order to find a coronet which is going to cause a national incident in two days, when the actual King of England turns up, and it's missing!"

Jessie's lips twitched into a smile as she watched her in the mirror and Flo felt the tension fall out of her, laughing and shaking her head.

"Oh, I don't know. The whole thing is ridiculous." She said, looking across at the American. "Rathbone doesn't seem to have paid any attention to security.

Anyone could have gained entry to the house and taken it."

"No forced doors or windows, though," Jessie reminded her.

"Probably because they were all left open with a big sign saying 'priceless treasure available to be stolen, please help yourself' above," Flo muttered bitterly.

"What about the butler?" Jessie asked.

Flo frowned, "The butler? The one who's sick?"

"Is he though? Seems a little convenient that he would be sick on the day the coronet disappears."

"You think he's hiding it in his bed sheets while pretending to have a fever?" Flo said, her tone making it clear how ridiculous she thought this idea was.

"I'm just saying I think we should check up on him in the morning. Check the story of all staff and guests, for that matter. Someone in this house either knows where the coronet is, or saw something that might give us an idea of what happened. We've just got to find out who."

"You make it sound easy," Flo grumbled, looking back at her reflection in the mirror and tugging at her hair with her fingers.

Why was it that Jessie could slump into an armchair and land with her dark bob in perfect order, her dressed not crumpled, and look as comfortable in her skin as she always did? Flo, on the other hand, only had to take a breath for her hair to become a frizzy mess of knots and tangles and her dress to ride up, overall giving the impression she had just fallen into a bush and climbed out again.

"That Mary Preston is quite something, don't you think?" Jessie said.

"If by 'something' you mean a snooty madam who looks down her nose at everyone else, then yes. I agree."

Jessie laughed before replying. "She does seem pretty unpleasant. I had the feeling she's angry at the world for some reason."

"Unlike our 'bright young things'," Flo said, rolling her eyes. "I think I could well be ready to hit Charles Becker on the nose before the weekends out."

"Then watch out for his sidekick, Beth. I'm pretty sure she'd scratch the eyes out of anyone who hurt the man she loves."

"It was fairly obvious, wasn't it?" Flo said, thinking back to how Beth Armstrong had always seemed to be at Charles's side, gazing up at him with her round brown eyes full of admiration.

"Then we have the rather drippy Ruth Robbins and the seemingly repressed Robert Pearce. But it's really Hector I find interesting."

Flo smirked, "Of course you do."

"Oh, don't get me wrong," Jessie smiled. "I'd gobble him up in a minute, but I meant I find his position here interesting."

"It's rather unusual, obviously, especially with him being at dinner." Flo mused, unsure what Jessie was getting at. "I think it's clear he cares about the animals and maybe it was his only way of staying in the country after his father died?"

"I wonder if..." Jessie's reply was cut short by a knock on the door.

"Come in," she called out, giving Flo a look filled with curiosity.

"Begging your pardon, ma'am," the housekeeper Evans said as she peered around the door, "But I thought it only right to come as soon as I heard. After all, Mr Rathbone said

The Tiger and the Coronet

we were to tell you anything we might know. Come along, girl!"

The speaker snapped this last comment at a young woman in a maid's outfit who hovered behind the housekeeper, wringing her apron.

"Ma'am, ma'am" She half nodded, half curtseyed to Jessie and Flo as she was pulled into the room by the housekeeper. Her eyes darted between them as everyone looked at her expectantly.

"Jenny here has got something to say about last night, haven't you Jenny?" the housekeeper Evans said.

The girl gave a jerky nod and looked down at her shoes.

"I'm sure it's not nothing important, but I told Cook and she told Mrs Evans, who said I should tell you."

"Go ahead then, Jenny," Flo said, smiling at the nervous girl.

The girl gave a thin smile back, swallowed, and began.

"Last night I woke up in a terrible sweat. I thought I might be getting sick like Mr Jenkins, so I got up to check the medicine cabinet for something when I heard this chattering from down the stairs. I had a peek through the door, not to spy or anything mind, I just wanted to check everything was alright."

"And who was it?" Jessie asked, her voice full of anticipation.

"It was Miss Armstrong and Mr Becker, ma'am. They had arms linked and were giggling something rotten."

"And where were they going?" Jessie continued eagerly.

"That's just it, ma'am," Jenny said, "they were heading down the corridor to The Gilt room."

Chapter Eight

"Are you sure we shouldn't wait?" Flo said as she jogged down the steps in front of Trelawny House to keep up with Jessie.

"Nonsense," Jessie replied with a dismissive flick of her hand, "If the rest of the house wants to lie about in their beds all day then let them, but it shouldn't stop us from starting our day."

It was only eight thirty in the morning, but Flo had to agree that it was bad form when hosting guests, or even if you were a guest yourself, to sleep in. They had, though, been assured by the housekeeper, Evans, that the house rarely rose much before nine. Unable to question the two people they most wanted to, Jessie had suggested they take a walk in the gardens and view the menagerie.

It was a warm, bright morning as they walked along the patterned brick path which ran along the edge of the main lawn. The sweet fragrance of the bright blue geraniums which were clustered along the left-hand edge of the path gave way to a more distinctly animal smell as they

The Tiger and the Coronet

approached the cluster of red bricked buildings, sheds and enclosures which formed the menagerie.

As they reached a wrought-iron gate set into a brick archway which marked the entrance, a flash of white caught Flo's eye. She bent down to the head of a geranium and picked off a ball of white cotton.

"How odd," she muttered, turning the ball in her fingers when she heard a sharp intake of breath from Jessie.

She looked up at Jessie's frozen figure, stood just beyond the archway. Her mouth hung slightly open, her eyes two rounded circles of shock, her face pale.

"Jessie, what is it?" Flo asked, moving through the archway towards her.

"Shh!" Jessie hissed, her right hand making a short, sharp cutting gesture while the rest of her stood stock still. Flo froze now too, her heart now hammering in her chest in alarm at the sudden change in her friend's normally cool exterior.

She turned her head slowly right, following Jessie's wide-eyed gaze with her own until it landed on a tiger. The seven foot long animal's head was bent to the ground, where it gnawed on the leg of Hector Diaz's clearly dead body. Flo involuntarily squeaked in alarm before slapping a hand over her own mouth..

She saw the beast's relaxed form stiffen and then raise its head towards them.

"Keep very still," Jessie whispered out of the side of her mouth.

Flo didn't need to be told. Her entire body had become as rigid as steel. A primal fear had taken root in her stomach as she stared into the enormous amber eyes now fixed on her.

She looked away quickly, as if looking into the animal's

eyes would be some kind of challenge, and tried to control her breathing as she took in the scene.

Hector was dead. There was no mistaking that. His young, lean body lay crookedly on the ground, his face in the dirt, arms outstretched above his head. His right leg was mostly missing, presumably in the tiger's stomach. She averted her eyes quickly to the thick bars of steel which were set into the front of a stone building to the right of the gruesome scene. The enclosures door stood wide open.

She heard a small gasp from Jessie on her left and turned back to the animal in front of them. It was moving now, slowly padding to their left around Hector's body.

"Quick!" Jessie shouted, shoving Flo violently to the right and bundling her through the open door of the enclosure. Flo stumbled before steadying herself and turning as Jessie slammed the cage door behind them, reached through the bars and slid the thick bolt across from the outside.

"What are you doing?!" Flo cried, despite her friend's actions being perfectly obvious to her.

"I'm trying to keep a certain amount of metal between us and a killer animal!" Jessie cried as she backed up to the rear wall.

Flo took a slow, deep breath, then another, trying to get her breathing under control.

"Yes," she said after a moment, "a fair point. How, though, do you expect us to ever get out again?"

The two women turned to look at each other, then back out through the bars. Outside the only exit stood the colossal form of the tiger, staring at them.

Chapter Nine

"Ok," Jessie whispered. "It's gone back to..." she paused for a moment before continuing, "What it was doing."

Flo swallowed, very much not trying to think of what the tiger had returned to doing.

"It's still too close to the door," she said, moving away from the rear wall of the enclosure for the first time. "We're going to need to find another way out of here."

She moved along the rear wall, staring at the solid red brick as though she could will a window, a hatch, or any other kind of escape to appear. When she reached the far side of the cage, she noted a recess cut in a line through the floor, running up one wall and across the ceiling. It culminated in a thick piece of steel which passed through two bars and extended out from the cage. She looked down and saw that it was sitting on a wooden trolley with four large wheels.

"This must be for separating the animal off if they need to get in the cage," she said as she pulled at the edge of the metal sheet and felt it slide towards her.

She looked out, but the tiger was not paying any attention. She pulled the metal sheet across to the far wall where it met the solid brick. No gap was left at the front, as she had hoped.

"There's no other way out," she said flatly.

"We could make a load of noise," Jessie suggested, "Hope someone from the house hears us?"

"Then we'd just be bringing more people to the bloody tiger!" Flo cried in an uncharacteristic outburst of annoyance.

"We're going to have to distract it away from the door and make a run for it," Jessie said. She turned her head, her eyes scanning the floor of the enclosure for anything they could use. She walked over to the middle of the back wall and bent down to a large metal dish full of water that was situated under a pipe which jutted out of the brickwork..

"This is obviously its water bowl, but I don't think that's going to do the job of distracting it. Where's its food bowl?"

The two women looked around the enclosure but saw nothing.

"I guess they just throw meat in through the bars," Jessie sighed and then suddenly stiffened as she looked back out through the bars. "Look," she hissed, "I think she's had enough."

Flo followed her gaze and saw the tiger turn away from Hector's body, pushing her powerful front legs forward in a stretch, before repeating the motion with her hind legs. The creature yawned and padded slowly to their right, away from the archway they had entered through and towards the other animal enclosures.

Jessie and Flo shared a hopeful look, both too afraid to speak in case they attracted the tiger back towards them. Slowly, both moved back towards the door of the cage and waited, peering in the direction the tiger had moved, but seeing and hearing nothing.

Flo's eyes were drawn, with a macabre dread, back to the body outside the cage door. Hector's long, toned arms were flung out towards them, as though in some last desperate request for help. She frowned.

"Are you ready?" Jessie said as she slowly slid the bolt across from the cage door.

"Yes" Flo nodded, taking a deep breath.

Jessie slowly swung the cage door open. They stepped outside... and ran.

Chapter Ten

"I can't believe this," Jessie said as they slowed to a fast walk halfway back to the house.

"I don't understand it," Flo said, glancing back at the archway to the menagerie. "Maybe Hector wasn't careful or made a mistake with the door or something but.." she trailed off.

Something was bothering her about the scene they had witnessed. Like an itch at the back of her brain. Something hadn't been quite right about it all. She shook her head and cursed herself mentally. Of course, something hadn't been right, a man was being eaten by a tiger!

"Flo!" Jessie said suddenly, making her jump back to reality. "Run!" Her friend screamed as she looked over her shoulder.

Flo turned to see the tiger, its loping walk carrying it through the archway and down the path towards them at a rapid pace.

She turned and ran up the steps to the house, bursting through the open door.

"Ah, there you are," Hugo Rathbone said as Flo and

The Tiger and the Coronet

Jessie slammed the front door behind them and leaned on it. "Off seeing the beasts, were we?"

'Make sure you shut all the doors and windows right now!' Jessie shouted at him." Jessie shouted at him.

He frowned back at her. He was wearing a silk embroidered dressing gown and held a cigarette in his left hand while Blue Boy perched on his right shoulder, his head bobbing excitedly.

"Oh, you don't need to worry about Blue boy here. He doesn't have any interest in the outside world," he chuckled.

"It's not to keep him in!" Jessie shouted. "it's to keep your damn tiger out!"

"Damn tiger!" Mimicked Blue Boy.

Hugo's mouth opened and then closed again, as the green baize door to the servants are of the house flew open and the housekeeper, Evans, appeared.

"Is everything ok, sir?" She said, clearly having been roused by the shouting.

"It's Mrs Evans, isn't it?" Flo said, trying to keep her voice calm.

"Yes miss," the woman replied with a confused frown on her face.

"Evans, Hector has been killed, and the tiger is loose. We must shut every door and window and make sure nobody leaves the house. Do you understand?"

The woman blinked her small round eyes a few times and then nodded with a quick "Yes, Miss." before scurrying back through the door.

Blue flapped his large wings and squawked several obscenities alongside 'Hector's dead! Hector's dead!'. Hugo's arm dropped, his cigarette and holder landing and rolling on the floor.

45

"Did you... Did you say Hector's dead?" He asked, his voice catching.

"Yes," Jessie answered, finally stepping away from the door. "I'm sorry."

Flo followed her to the hall window and looked out. The tiger was pacing across the lawn, its head moving from side to side as it surveyed its expanded world.

"We need to send for help," Flo said, turning back to Hugo, who had followed them to the window and was now staring in horror at his pet killing machine through the glass. "Do you have a telephone?"

He nodded slowly, "Yes, behind the stairs there," He said gesturing.

"Do you have an animal expert you use, maybe a vet who comes to the menagerie?"

"No, I..." he paused and shook his head. "Hector takes care of all that." He paled some more. "Took care of it," he corrected himself.

"In that case," Jessie said, "Maybe you should phone the local police. If that thing gets into the town, who knows what it will do."

"Yes, yes, of course," Hugo said, turning towards the phone cupboard. "Her name's Duchess, you know," he said quietly as he walked away.

"Are you ok?" Jessie said, turning to Flo and taking both her hands in her own.

Flo blew out her cheeks. "I think so, you?"

Jessie nodded, "I just can't believe it," she sighed. "I guess if you work with dangerous animals for so long, something like this is bound to happen. Maybe you become complacent."

Flo gasped as realisation struck her.

"Flo? What is it?" Jessie asked, her brow furrowing in concern.

"There was something not quite right about all this, and I think I've just realised what it is."

"Good morning."

They turned to see Thaddeus Barnes descending the stairs. He pulled a pocket watch from the breast of his jacket and looked at the time.

"Do you know if breakfast is being served yet? I know Hugo's not much of a morning person, but I'm famished."

Jessie began to explain the situation, but paused when she saw other guests apparelling at the top of the stairs.

"Why don't we gather everyone in the dining room," she said, looking at Flo.

She nodded and Jessie began asking everyone to follow her as Flo saw Hugo leaving the phone cupboard and hurried over to him.

"They're going to try to find someone who can help," he said, his voice think with emotion. "In the meantime, they're going to position armed men on the boundary of the estate. I told them," he raised his finger, suddenly angry, "If any of them shoots Duchess I will have them thrown in jail for murder!"

Chapter Eleven

By the time Hugo had calmed down enough for Flo to lead him to the dining room, it was clear that Jessie had already passed on the unhappy news.

Flo studied the faces that turned to them as they entered the room.

Charles Becker stood with his arm around Elizabeth Armstrong nest to the sideboard where breakfast was laid out. She was sobbing quietly.

Ruth Robbins sat wide-eyed and pale next to Mary Preston, who was placing a cigarette in her holder and lighting it with shaking hands.

Thaddeus Barnes stared at his hands placed on the white tablecloth in front of him, while next to him, Robert Pearce sat stony faced.

"Is it true Hugo?" Charles asked.

"I'm afraid so, old boy," he said in a hoarse voice as he made his way over to the drinks cabinet.

"But how is it possible, for goodness sake?" Charles continued. "I thought the cage was never opened?"

"The only time it's ever opened," Hugo said as he poured himself a large whisky. "Is when Hector cleaned the enclosure out. Before that, he would leave her some meat at the far end, which can be separated from the rest of the enclosure from the outside. He'd never have opened the door unless she was secured in the holding pen first."

"Maybe he thought he had?" Thadd said, lifting his head for the first time. "Maybe he thought the thing was shut in at the end, but it wasn't secure?"

"No," Hugh replied, shaking his head. "It's a sliding sheet of metal two inches thick that goes across the enclosure. It would be obvious if the thing wasn't closed all the way, let alone if there was a big enough gap for Duchess to get through."

"Maybe he'd been drinking?" Charles offered, which for some reason made Elizabeth sob again as she put her head on his chest.

"Whatever the cause, it's just a terrible accident," Robert said, removing his glasses to clean them on a napkin.

"The police are going to keep her contained to the grounds while we wait for someone who can come and sedate her," Hugo explained to the group. "Until then, we have to remain in the house, obviously."

"I assume there's no way the thing can get in the house?" Charles asked.

"Evans is taking care of that, I believe," said Hugo. "All windows and doors shut, etc."

"Did any of you see Hector this morning, or visit the menagerie?" Flo asked.

There was a moment of silence as a look of shock passed across many of the gathered faces.

"Why would you ask such a thing?" Thadd said, clearly

speaking for the sentiment in the room. "Are you implying that one of us was fool enough to go and let the tiger out?!"

"I'm just trying to establish a timeline for when this might have happened," Flo answered in a voice far more calm than she felt. She turned to Hugo. "You said that the only time Hector would open the door is when he cleared out the enclosure. Do you know when he did that? Was there a schedule?"

"I'm sorry, I have no idea," Hugo answered with a frown. "I never paid much attention to how it all worked. It was never this early though, I'm fairly sure of that. Hector is about as much of a morning person as I am." He gave a small laugh, which died in his throat as he looked down. "Was, I mean," he finished quietly.

"What about last night," Flo continued, "Did anyone see him?" She paused here, suddenly realising the implications of what she was about to say.

"Did anyone see him again after we'd all gone to bed," Jessie said, picking up on Flo's thread, but with far less prudishness.

There was a general smattering of denials from the group before people began talking amongst themselves and continuing their breakfast,

"What did you think?" Jessie asked in a low voice as the two of them stood in a corner of the room.

"I think that none of this makes sense," Flo answered. "Hugo said that Hector had grown up working with animals. Would he really make a mistake, like opening the cage door when the tiger was loose?"

"He looked as though he'd been dead a while," Jessie added. "I don't think he could have died this morning."

Flo's lips thinned as she looked about, ensuring that

nobody was listening to them. "Did you notice his arms?" She said quietly.

"His arms?"

She nodded. "They didn't have a scratch on them."

Jessie frowned uncomprehendingly, then her eyes widened to circles. "Wait, if the tiger had attacked him, he would have tried to defend himself."

"Exactly. He would have punched, kicked, screamed, done whatever it took to get the thing off him or hurt it, but I couldn't see any wounds at all. Only on his leg where..." She paused and Jessie nodded. Neither of them wanted to revisit that image.

"So what does that mean? You think he was maybe dead before the tiger started... you know what?" Jessie asked.

The two young women gave each other a long, meaningful look before Jessie turned away and called out to Hugo.

As he approached, Flo saw that some of the colour had returned to his long, thin face, but he still looked deeply troubled.

"I'm so sorry," he said as he reached them. "I don't quite know what to do."

"I think that's understandable in the circumstances," Flo said softly. "And there's not a lot we can do for now. The police will bring someone in to deal with soon, I'm sure."

"In fact," Jessie said, cutting in. "There is one thing."

They both looked at her expectantly.

"I'm afraid, despite the tragedy of this morning, the coronet is still missing."

"Oh god," Hugo said, looking down at his feet.

"We'd like to talk to everyone in the house individually

so we can get a picture of where everyone was on the night it went missing."

Hugo's eyes widened for a moment before he frowned and nodded. "Yes, yes, quite right. You can use my study to talk to people. Will you want to talk to the staff?"

"Yes," Jessie answered, looking up and across the room's occupants, "but I think we'll start with your guests."

Chapter Twelve

Beth Armstrong's eyes were still ringed with red when she entered the wood panelled study half an hour later. She clung to Charles Becker's arm, much as she had done in the breakfast hall.

"We were told you wanted to see us?" Charles said, chin raised. Flo had the impression that, although slightly annoyed about being summoned in this way, he had been expecting it.

"Yes," Jessie said, "We thought, in light of this morning's events, it was time to put this nonsense about the coronet to bed. Don't you?"

Beth gave a gasp as her hands tightened together on her lap.

"Now look," Charles said, leaning forward in his chair, his expression serious. "I'm not sure what you're implying, but we have had nothing to do with any of this business."

"We're not sure that's true," Flo said in a steady tone.

"Oh, Charles!" Beth said, turning to him, "They know!"

"Be quiet Beth!" He hissed back at her, his cheeks reddening.

"But it's all our fault, Charles! It's our fault he's dead!" Beth wailed as she descended into more sobs.

Flo took a sharp intake of breath in shock as she turned to Jessie, who looked just as taken aback as she was.

The maid had told them she had seen Charles and Beth heading to The Gilt room late at night, and Jessie and Flo had both been of the opinion that the two of them had taken the coronet as a prank or joke of some kind, but Hector's death? What did that have to do with anything?

"She's very upset," Charles said. "She doesn't know what she's saying. I think I should take her to her room to rest."

"We know the two of you went to The Gilt room on Friday night after everybody had gone to bed," Jessie said.

There was a thick silence, as even Beth's tears halted in shock.

"For goodness sake," Charles said angrily, "Damn staff should mind their own business. Which one of them was it?"

"I think you should focus on explaining what you were doing in The Gilt room at that time of night rather than worrying about which staff member to shout at," Jessie said.

Charles looked shocked for a moment, and then angry. He looked at the two women opposite him and then spoke in a tight voice.

"We don't have to explain anything to you," he said, rising from his seat. "Beth is clearly upset, and you treating us like criminals is hardly helping. Come on Beth," he took her arm and guided her out of her seat and towards the door, moving her into the hallway in front of him before turning back to them one last time.

"We had nothing to do with the coronet going missing and nothing to do with Hector's accident." And then, with the door slamming behind him, he was gone.

"Well," Jessie said. "Whatever I was expecting, it wasn't that."

"Same here," Flo said thoughtfully. "Is it just me, or does Beth seem far more upset than she should for the accidental death of a man she barely knew?"

"Definitely," Jessie replied. "Not to mention that she seems to be worried that we would blame them for his death." She turned to Flo, her grey eyes alive with curiosity. "So, what do you think?"

Flo sighed. "With the two of them being involved in the Bright Young Things, I was sure this was just some sort of elaborate prank. That's what they do isn't it? Cause chaos and silliness for their own amusement?"

"Pretty much," Jessie said, smiling.

"Well, if this was them playing a joke, they don't seem to be finding it funny anymore."

"But why?" Jessie asked. "Did it get out of hand somehow?" She gave a sudden gasp. "Maybe Hector had discovered they had stolen it, so they decided to bump him off before he could rat them out?"

"We don't know that anyone bumped Hector off. There could have been an innocent explanation for the lack of wounds he had. In any case, I think it's more likely they would have just laughed it off as a prank, don't you?"

For a moment, Jessie looked slightly disappointed at the dismissing of her theory, but then brightened. "Unless the whole prank aspect was just a backup."

"A backup?" Flo said with a frown. "What do you mean?"

"What if they actually wanted to steal the coronet, for real I mean? To, oh I don't know, sell on or whatever."

"Ok," Flo said slowly, still not following.

"Everyone knows they're jokesters, so if they get caught with the thing, they can just say it was all for a bit of fun. Hand the thing back to Hugo and no one ever suspects they were really trying to get the thing. If they don't get caught," she shrugged, "Well, they get away with it."

Flo thought about this for a moment before nodding. "That's not actually a bad theory, but why would they even want to steal the coronet? Neither of them are short of money, are they?"

"Maybe not, but greed is a terrible thing."

"How would you even go about selling something like that?" Flo asked. "Who would even want it?"

"Oh, you'd be surprised," Jessie said. "There are people out there who want famous paintings or objects precisely because they are famous. Some of them are even stolen to order. Of course, if they didn't actually want the coronet themselves and someone hadn't paid them to get it, they could always melt the thing down. Much easier to move a lump of gold and some gems than it is a coronet."

Flo stared at her.

"What?" Jessie said defensively. "I just pick up things, don't look at me like that! Let's speak to the next person. Who do you think?"

"I've no idea," Flo admitted with a small sigh. "Charles and Beth were the only lead we had, and we've ended up with more questions than when they came in here. Let's just see who I find first." She rose from her chair and headed out into the hallway.

In the far corner, the tall, slender figure of Mary Preston

stood. She faced the housekeeper Evans. In her elegant hand was a telegram.

"I'm so sorry Miss Preston," Evans said, "It came in yesterday but with Mr Jenkins being ill, one of the maids took it into the kitchen and the silly girl plum forgot."

Mary didn't answer, didn't really seem to even hear her. She just stared at the telegram in her hands. After a moment, Evans moved away uncertainly, glancing at Flo before vanishing through the baize door which led to the kitchens.

"Mary?" Flo called out as she approached slowly.

The woman spun around, screwing up the telegram along with the envelope it had been delivered in as she did so.

"Miss Hammond," she said cooly, "how can I help you?"

"Call me Flo, please," she answered, feeling now awkward at having called her by her first name, despite this being the norm at Trelawny House. "Jessie and I were wondering if we could have a word in private."

Mary eyed her, her almost too perfect, porcelain like features angled slightly upwards in judgment.

"Of course," she answered, moving across the hall and throwing the paper she held into the fire grate set into the wall.

"Just in the study," Flo gestured to the door and followed Mary to it. As the taller woman opened and moved inside the room with a cat-like grace, Flo darted back across the hall. She bent, grabbed the paper from the grate and stuffed it into the pocket of her cardigan before hurrying back to the study and entering.

Chapter Thirteen

Mary Preston sat in upright elegance in the chair opposite them. Her hair curled at her shoulder, her doleful eyes focused and unconcerned.

"Can we hurry this along?" she said in the cut glass tones of the aristocracy. "I didn't take the coronet and I don't know who did."

"You think someone took it, though?" Flo said.

Mary Preston's gaze bore into her.

"I thought finding who took it was what you were here to do?"

"It may have simply been misplaced," Flo countered.

Mary gave a contemptuous eye roll.

"I hardly think you're going to find it's rolled under a sideboard, do you?"

"You saw the coronet on the night it went missing, though?" Jessie asked.

"Of course," Mary answered with a sigh of boredom, "Hugo was passing it around as though it was just some interesting bauble."

"You think he was being careless?" Flo asked.

Mary gave a mirthless laugh. "I wouldn't trust Hugo to look after a rock, let alone a country's priceless heirloom."

"You think he's untrustworthy?"

"Hugo?" she answered, for the first time looking slightly confused by the question put to her, "he's not untrustworthy, the man hasn't the guile to be untrustworthy. He's..." she looked up, as though seeking the right words, "not someone you would say has moral responsibility."

Flo felt a jolt of interest pass through her. "That's an interesting turn of phrase."

Mary sighed again and leaned forward, placing her hands on the desk that sat between them. "Look, Hugo brought the coronet in. Everyone passed it around and said the appropriate words about how fantastic it was, then he put it away. That's it."

"Did you see him put it away?" Jessie asked.

"No, we were all in the sitting room and he left with it. I assume he took back to the safe in The Gilt room. I really can't tell you anymore than that, so I assume I'm done here?"

"What was your relationship with Hector Diaz?"

Flo wasn't sure why she asked it. She had no reason to as far as she was aware, but something in the back of her mind was nagging her that Hector's death and the coronet's disappearance were connected.

"What do you mean, relationship? I had no relationship with Hector."

She had answered too quickly, too forcefully, it seemed to Flo.

"You didn't see him last night after everyone had gone to bed?"

"Of course not, what a ridiculous question." Mary's

normally pale complexion had warmed to a soft pink. "Obviously what's happened was a terrible accident, but I don't see what it has to do with me or the blasted coronet."

"Nor do we," Flo said calmly. "That's why we're asking these questions."

"Well," Mary said, rising from her chair and looking down at them imperiously, "you're done asking them to me." She turned, opened the door, and strode out into the hall.

Flo stood up, walked to the door, and closed it gently before fishing in her pocket for the paper she had pulled out of the grate.

"What's that?" Jessie asked in a curious tone.

"A telegram," Flo answered as she unfolded it and began reading. "Take action now, stop. Reward is waiting. Stop. Just need to grasp it, stop."

"Well, that's very interesting," Jessie said. "I wonder what on earth it means?"

"It's obviously someone who knows she's here, as that's where the telegram has come, and it's sounds like its someone who knows she is here for a purpose."

"A purpose like stealing a coronet?"

There was a loud rap on the door. Flo jumped before stuffing the telegram back in her pocket and calling out for whoever it was to come in.

Thaddeus Barnes entered and closed the door behind him. He walked over to them, looked down them, hair swept back and moustache bristling.

"I believe you are speaking to all guests at Trelawny, and I thought I would offer up my side of things." He looked behind him back towards the door and continued in a lower tone of voice, bending down towards them, "I understand you may have heard certain things which could, incorrectly, throw suspicion on myself in light of the coronet's disappearance." He stood up straighter again and his voice returned to normal volume. "I am a firm believer in tackling things head on when possible."

"Then you'd better sit down," Flo said, gesturing to the chair and trying not to sound as bewildered as she felt over this information.

Chapter Fourteen

Thadd sat opposite them and placed his hands on the desk between them, fingers interlaced. He gave Flo the impression of someone who had seen men of importance speak and desperately wanted to imitate them.

As he opened his mouth to begin his explanation of recent events, Jessie cut him off.

"We're glad you came. We've obviously heard some things which have, unfortunately, placed you high on our possible list of suspects for the theft of the coronet."

Flo glanced at the woman sitting next to her in surprise, but Jessie did not meet her gaze. Instead, she stared at the man across from them with an intensity that quickly did its work.

"I see," Thadd said, slumping slightly in his chair. "Hugo has already told you. Well, quite right I suppose, quite right."

"Can you run us through it in your own words please," jessie continued, not missing a beat.

Thadd looked up again, and this time his eyes weren't

focused and businesslike. They were sad and, Flo thought, a little pleading.

"I can assure you, I did not take the coronet. I realise it doesn't look good, but I would never threaten my country's political ambitions. Hugo knows that, and he knows that I told those men, very firmly, that they had no business here."

"As I said, please, just walk us through it. Hugo told us everything, he had to, but we'd like to hear it from you," Jessie said in a level tone.

Thadd sighed and leaned back in his chair.

"I owe some people some money," he said simply with a shrug. "It didn't even occur to me that those goons would come here. They're from Cardiff, sent by the people I owe money to. Unfortunately," he said with a wan smile, "I like to gamble. Always have. I've had a bit of a losing streak that's got away from me a little." He rubbed his face in his hands. "They thought that if I was staying here, they might be able to lean on me to rip off poor old Hugo."

"They wanted you to steal from him?" Flo asked.

"As good as," Thadd answered, "They wanted me to persuade him to pay off my debts. Obviously I refused, which is what I told Hugo after he'd seen me talking to the rather unsavoury characters outside the house. Of course, Hugo offered to help me out in any case. That's who he is, an honourable man."

"So you have no reason to have stolen the coronet if Hugo has taken care of your issues." Jessie said.

"I didn't take his offer!" Thadd snapped back, bolting upright with indignation in his voice. "As kind as it was, I would never burden a friend with problems which are mine alone to solve."

"Do you think these men could have returned and taken the coronet?" Jessie continued.

Thadd's brow knitted. "These men were nothing more than street thugs. I very much doubt they would have had the brain capacity to have conceived of such a plan. In any case, nobody outside of the people in this house knows the coronet is here."

"Nobody?" Flo asked, slightly surprised.

"Well, of course the British authorities are aware, and the local police force etc." He trailed off, frowning again at his own words.

"Who all have families and friends who no doubt love some juicy gossip," Jessie said, raising her eyebrows at Flo.

"I am sure that these people are professionals," Thadd said, "and this would have been treated with the utmost of security and secrecy."

Jessie gave a snort of laughter. "Yeah, until they'd had a few pints down their local pub."

"In any case," Thadd continued, undeterred, "I'm sure Hugo has told you there were no signs of a break in."

"With all due respect," Jessie said, still smiling, "Hugo doesn't seem the conscientious sort, particularly where security is concerned."

Thadd looked down and took a deep breath, as though in acknowledgement of this fact. "Look," he said, "I'm telling you I had nothing to do with the coronet going missing. Part of me thinks it really has just been misplaced somewhere, but..."

"But, what?" Flo asked eagerly.

"The guests here," he said quietly, "Hugo is too trusting and too ready to accept people if you ask me."

"What do you mean by that?"

"He doesn't really know any of these people you know. Well, except me and Ruth, obviously. Somehow they've managed to invite themselves to Trelawny House right at one of the most historical moments in its long history."

"Surely they weren't strangers to him, though?" Jessie asked.

"Near enough," Thadd snorted. "Robert Pearce sent him a telegram out of the blue. The man was a low level accountant before he inherited wealth from some distant relative who Hugo knew. Now he's trying to learn the life of the nobility. Like some sort of blinking mole who's burst from the ground and now wants to learn to fly. Charles and Beth were much the same. Used some friend of a friend by way of introduction, but basically forced their way in here by letter. I think they've only met Hugo once or twice when he's been in London, and that in passing. It's Mary Preston who takes the cake, though. She didn't send any communication at all, just turned up!"

"She just arrived at the house?" Flo asked, shocked at the idea of this lack of social etiquette.

"She arrived in town and booked herself into a hotel. She'd only been there one night before she called at Trelawny, talking about how her father and Hugo were old acquaintances, etc. Of course, Hugo being Hugo, he invited her to stay immediately."

"And do you have any reason to suspect these people of ulterior motives for coming here?"

"I would have thought that was rather obvious, wasn't it? Hugo is an immensely rich, generous and slightly gullible man who thinks the best of everybody. Who better to come leech a few pounds off, and you get free room and board as well?"

There was another knock on the door and Thadd jumped like a schoolboy being caught with his hand in the biscuit tin.

"Anyway," he said, rising from his chair, "It's not for me to discuss Hugo's guests, they can explain themselves. I assume this is another of them now, so I'll leave you to get on."

He hurried to the door, opened it, nodded to a startled looking Robert Pearce and left.

"Come on Robert," Ruth Robbins said, coming in from the hall and taking his arm in hers, "It's time to face the inquisition!"

Chapter Fifteen

"I hear we're the last to be seen," Ruth said as they sat down. "And I'm sure you've saved the best for last."

"Oh, really?" Flo said, looking at the two. Robert had taken his round glasses off and was cleaning them with a cloth he'd taken from his pocket, revealing his small, round, red-rimmed eyes. He looked as out of place and nervous as he had throughout the short time they had known him. Ruth also had the same languid, dreamy, calm she seemed to always sport.

"Robert here has something that might well shed light on this little mystery, not that it's very mysterious, really."

"Oh?" Flo said, looking at Robert.

He placed his round glasses back on his face, and his eyes resumed their magnified look.

He licked his lips as he looked at them both briefly before returning his gaze to the desktop.

"It was a little hot in my room on Friday night, and it woke me. I went to open the window, and I saw," he stopped and swallowed before continuing, "I saw Charles and Beth heading along the path towards the menagerie."

He wrung his hands as Jessie and Flo exchange a glance.

"I think it's pretty obvious they were up to some high jinx knowing their reputation," Ruth said. "It wouldn't surprise me at all if they had squirrelled the coronet away as some great joke."

"And you think they hid it in the menagerie?" Flo asked, her heart now racing.

Ruth's eyebrows rose. "Well, that would make sense."

"Have you told anyone else this?" Flo asked Robert.

"He's only told me," Ruth answered for him. "I thought it best we came and tell you right away."

"And why didn't you come forward with this before now?" Jessie asked.

"Oh, I, um..." Robert stammered in his high voice.

"I think Robert thought the obvious," Ruth laughed. "That they were headed out there for some sort of lover's tryst."

"I didn't like to pry into private matters," Robert said with a sheepish smile.

"But surely, once you knew the coronet was missing?" Jessie said.

"It all felt a little accusatory," Robert answered, "But in light of Hector's death."

Flo felt Jessie's eyes flick to her and asked the obvious question. "You think they might have had something to do with his death?"

"Oh, no!" Robert cried, looking appalled at the idea. "I just wondered if they might have seen something that shed light on the whole business. If they had gone there again at night to, well," his round face flushed again.

"Can I ask where you were on the night the coronet disappeared?" Flo said, turning to Ruth.

The Tiger and the Coronet

"Oh, tucked up in bed, I'm afraid and saw and heard nothing. Missed anything exciting, rotten luck," she gave a dreamy sigh.

"And last night?" Flo asked, looking between them.

"Last night?" Ruth asked, "Same again, I'm afraid."

Flo's eyes flicked to Robert.

"I went to bed too. I didn't hear anything out of the ordinary."

"Can I ask what you make of the other guests here at Trelawny?" Jessie asked.

"I'm afraid I only really know Thadd," Ruth said. "I'm not sure I care much for the others, though."

"Why do you say that?" Jessie pressed.

"Oh, I don't know. Charles and Elizabeth can be quite mean and Mary swans about as though she's queen."

Flo and Jessie looked at Robert expectantly.

"I don't like to speak ill of others if I can help it," He said quietly.

"And that's why Robert's alright," Ruth said with a grin. "He's a kind soul. A little too trusting if you ask me, though. Do you know he's brought an extraordinary amount of cash with him, five hundred pounds?"

Flo let out an involuntary gasp at the thought of this huge sum.

"I know! Just laying about in his room," she smiled at Robert and he smiled sheepishly back at her.

The door opened, and Hugo Rathbone's thin face appeared. "excuse me, sorry to disturb and all that, but I was wondering if I could have a word?"

"Yes, of course," Flo said. "We were just finishing up, anyway."

Ruth and Robert stood and exchanged pleasantries with Hugo as they left.

The Viscount sat heavily in the chair opposite them. He had finally dressed for the day, but his appearance was slightly dishevelled. His jaw showed the slightest signs of stubble, and his tie was poorly done and slightly askew.

"Have you spoken to everyone now?" He asked, "I've been sending them all over to you."

"We have," Flo answered, "apart from the staff, who we'll get to next."

"Right, good. I don't suppose anyone's owned up to taking the coronet, have they?"

"I'm afraid not."

He nodded glumly, "Of course. Well, we still have a couple of days before the king arrives and I'm declared a buffoon in the eyes of the world." He gave a thin smile, but his eyes weren't in it. "I'm afraid things aren't much better on the Duchess front."

Flo had to think for a minute to remember that he was talking about the tiger named Duchess, and not some other royal visitor due to visit.

"In what way? Is everyone ok?" Jessie asked, clearly fearing some further incident with the animal.

"Oh no, nothing like that," Hugo said quickly to reassure her. "It's just that I've had a call back from the police and the earliest some sort of tiger expert can get here is Tuesday."

"Tuesday!" Flo exclaimed, shocked at the idea of the tiger being allowed to roam the grounds for another forty-eight hours.

"They've tried every vet in South Wales, but all their tranquillisers are given by syringe. Even the most hardened veterinarian balks at trying to get close enough to a tiger for that. They need a gun, with special darts that deliver the stuff to knock the old girl out."

"Aren't they worried she will leave the estate, get into town or into a farmer's field with livestock?" Jessie asked.

"They are," Hugo said grimly. "The blighters are insisting they'll shoot her on site if she does." His face brightened somewhat. "I have a plan for that though. Evans should be seeing to it now."

Chapter Sixteen

"No sign of her yet, Mr Rathbone," the diminutive housekeeper said, turning as Hugo, Jessie and Flo entered the upper floor bedroom.

"And how much did you put out?" Hugo asked, moving alongside her at the open window and peering out.

"Two steaks and a whole chicken. I thought that would be enough to keep her happy for a while."

Flo and Jessie moved over to the window as well, and looking down, saw the meat laying in the grass below them.

"You're throwing down food for her?" Jessie asked, incredulous.

"Of course," Hugo said, as though this was the most normal thing in the world. "It's better for me to feed her and keep her here than she goes off, causes trouble, and gets herself shot."

Jessie opened her mouth to reply, but then closed it again as she looked thoughtfully back out the window.

"It does mean you're encouraging her to stay around the house and expect meat though," Flo said quietly.

Hugo blanched slightly as they all stared out of the window, looking for signs of Duchess.

"If you don't need anything else, sir," Evans said, "I'd best be getting back to my duties."

"Quite right, Evans, thank you."

"Actually," Flo said, causing the woman to pause as she moved towards the door, "Could we have a quick word?"

The housemaid looked towards her employer.

"Oh, of course, yes. Please help in any way you can, Evans. That goes for the rest of the staff as well."

"Yes, sir," she nodded, "Would you mind talking while we walk? I need to check on Mr Jenkins."

"Is that the butler?" Flo asked.

"That's right Miss."

"If it's ok, we'd like to speak with him as well."

"Very well, Miss," Evans nodded and headed out of the bedroom with Flo and Jessie in tow. "He's still not himself, but he seems much brighter this morning."

"Do you know what was wrong with him?" Jessie asked as they walked.

"I don't know, Miss, it was all very strange. I've never known him to have so much as a sniffle in all the years I've known him. Then, yesterday morning, he couldn't even get out of bed!"

"What were the symptoms?" Flo asked.

"Oh, he was bad. He was sick and shaking and we couldn't get him warm for the longest time. Then he slept most of yesterday. He seems much brighter today, but he's still got a headache and seems weaker than his normal self."

"Did you notice anything unusual on the night the coronet went missing?" Jessie asked as they turned right into another hallway.

"Oh no Miss," Evans answered quickly, "I couldn't

believe it when I heard the coronet was gone, and then when young Jenny told me she'd seen two of the guests heading that way, I didn't know what to think! I just knew you were here to look into the thing and Mr Rathbone had said to help you in any way we could."

She paused at a small, green baize door set into the wall. "Are you sure you want to see him now and not when he's feeling better and up and about?"

"I think we'd rather see him now if that's ok?" Flo said.

"Of course, Miss," she replied, but her expression seemed to suggest that them entering the servants' quarters was an imposition.

She led them up a narrow staircase which opened out onto a central corridor which ran away from them with doors on either side. They moved down it, only stopping at the very end room situated on the left. Evans gave a sharp rap on the door and a male voice called for them to come in.

Inside, the air was stale, the light dim with the only window being a closed skylight in the sloping roof which ran away to their right. The room contained only a side table and a bed with a thin, pale man sat upright in it. He was wearing white and blue striped pyjamas, and his eyes widened as he saw Jessie and Flo entering behind Evans.

"Mr Jenkins," Evans said in a soft voice, "these two ladies would like to have a word with you."

"Mrs Evans!" The man replied in an incredulous but weak voice. "I hardly think it is appropriate for you to bring ladies into these quarters!"

"I'm sorry, Mr Jenkins," Flo said hurriedly, seeing the surprisingly stricken look on the normally flat-faced Evans. "I'm afraid we insisted. It is rather important."

The thin man's lips pursed and then flattened into a line. His face had a rather squashed appearance under a bald head that sported hair at either side, just above his ears.

"Very well...?" He said, leaving the unspoken question hanging.

"My name is Flo Hammond, and this is Jessie Circle."

The man bowed his head towards them. "It's very nice to meet you, Miss. If I had known you needed to speak to me so urgently, I would, of course, come downstairs." At this, he gave another sharp glance to the housekeeper.

"We won't take up much of your time," Jessie said, "especially as you've been unwell."

"I'm feeling much better now thank you miss. I'll be back on my feet in no time."

"You became ill on Friday, is that right?" Flo asked, "On the night the coronet went missing?"

"That's right, Miss," Jenkins said, a pained look passing across his face. "If I had been well, I'm sure it would never have happened. I always make sure the doors locked once the house has gone to bed."

"I assure you," Evans said hotly, "the doors were locked!"

"Yes, well," Jenkins said, "I also normally sleep on the ground floor, so I'm sure I would have heard any shenanigans."

"But you slept up here that night?" Flo said, looking around the rather bare room. It certainly didn't look like a room anyone lived in.

"That's right Miss, we use this room when someone is taken ill."

Flo frowned at that, but didn't want to derail the conversation.

"And what time were you taken ill?"

"Oh, it was mid-afternoon, I believe, but I'm afraid everything is a little hazy."

"Did you eat or drink anything unusual that day?" Jessie asked.

The man looked at her in puzzlement before sharing a glance with the housekeeper.

"Nothing out of the ordinary Miss, we all had lunch in the kitchen as normal."

Evans cleared her throat, causing them all to turn to her.

"There was the drink you shared with Mr Becker," she said with eyebrows raised.

"Oh, well, I'm sure the ladies didn't mean something like that."

"You had a drink with Charles Becker?" Flo asked, the skin on the back of her neck prickling with anticipation.

"Mr Becker was kind enough to share a glass of a new port he had acquired," Jenkins said with a frown. "It was very generous of him."

"Downright odd, if you ask me," Evans muttered.

"Mrs Evans!" The butler exclaimed in shock.

"I'm just saying," Evans said, "he offers you a drink and then you're poorly after and he was sneaking around that night. Young Jenny saw him."

Jenkins's eyes bulged from his head. "Mrs Evans, please! This kind of gossip is inappropriate!"

"I just don't know what's going on anymore," Evan's continued, unabashed, "We've got crowns being stolen, people skulking about at night, pills going missing and now poor Mr Diaz is dead and eaten by the tiger!"

There was a knock on the door and the voice of Jenny the maid could be heard from the corridor outside.

"Mrs Evans?"

The Tiger and the Coronet

The housekeeper opened the door to the wide-eyed maid.

"What is it Jenny? Can't you see we're busy?"

The young girl looked over the housekeeper's shoulder and took a step back in horror at the idea of two house guests crammed in the small room with Mr Jenkins and his striped pyjamas.

"I...I'm sorry, Mrs Evans, but there's an awful fight going on and we didn't know what to do!"

Chapter Seventeen

They heard the commotion as soon as they left the stairs leading to the attic. An angry male voice rose from the stairs as they hurried towards the sound.

"How did you do it?" Charles Becker shouted as they moved down the wide staircase. "Did you swoop in when the old man was ill without any of us knowing?"

He was leaning, red-faced, towards a pale Robert Pearce. His mouth so close that Flo was surprised his breath wasn't steaming up Robert's glasses.

"I never met him at all!" Robert protested in his high pitch voice.

"Ha! And you expect me to believe that?"

Beth Armstrong and Ruth Robbins stood watching the scene in silence as Robert Pearce glanced pleadingly at Flo and Jessie as they reached the bottom of the stairs with Evans in tow.

"What on earth's going on here?" Jessie asked.

"This weasel," Charles snarled, jabbing a finger into Robert's chest, "stole my inheritance!"

The Tiger and the Coronet

"I did no such thing!" Robert spluttered.

"Maybe you falsified the will," Charles said. "I told that bloody lawyer something funny had gone on."

"Charles," Jessie said, walking to him and taking his arm, "why don't we move to the drawing room, get you a drink, and you can explain what's going on?" She turned to Flo. "Why don't you take Robert to the library for the same?"

Flo nodded and began to escort the bewildered-looking man across the hall in the opposite direction.

Chapter Eighteen

Beth had followed Jessie and Charles into the drawing room, as Jessie knew she would.

"Beth, darling, would you mind making some drinks for us all?"

"Oh, of course," the young woman said, looking pleased at being able to do something rather than just stand and watch.

Charles perched on the edge of a sofa, hands clasped, his body still tense. Jessie sat next to him and spoke softly.

"So, let's start with whose inheritance you were talking about, shall we?"

Charles sighed heavily and rubbed his face with his hands.

"Victor Saltern," he replied gruffly before taking the drink Beth offered him and drinking deeply.

"He was my..." he faltered, as though unsure of his choice of words. "He was a close friend of my family. Practically raised me after my father died. I was only 9 when it happened and there he was, just a stranger then, of course. Came to give his condolences and see if he could do anything for my mother, but it was me he really helped. He took me fishing, shooting. Sometimes we'd just walk and talk. As I got older, he began to show me his estate, how things worked, how to run the place."

"He was a wealthy man, then?"

Charles snorted. "He was not that he ever cared about that. He was an old-fashioned kind of chap. Cared about his tenants, cared about the land." He took another drink and stared at the floor. "I thought he cared about me, but when he died last year, I found out the truth."

"I take it that you weren't named in his will?"

"Do you know, in all the years I knew him, he never mentioned having a brother? Not once."

Jessie waited for him to continue, but the young man had a far away look in his hazel eyes.

"His brother was the main beneficiary?" She prompted.

Charles gave a bitter laugh.

"No, that would have made more sense in a way. His brother had died five years earlier from the same heart issue that did for him in the end."

Chapter Nineteen

Flo and Robert positioned themselves on armchairs in the long, narrow library as Ruth addressed the drinks trolley.

"Are you ok?" Flo asked. "He didn't hurt you at all?"

"Oh. No, no," Robert replied, taking off his thick glasses and cleaning them with a handkerchief from his jacket pocket. "I can understand why he's angry, I'm afraid. I've been wrestling with some guilt over all this myself."

"Charles said something about an inheritance?"

Robert nodded and thanked Ruth as she passed him a drink. "Yes, I was fortunate enough to receive an inheritance last year from my estranged uncle."

"Estranged?" Flo asked.

"Well," Robert hesitated, "estranged might not be the right word in relation to me. I'm afraid a never knew of him at all until five years ago when my father died suddenly, his heart gave out. It was only once I was dealing with his various papers that I discovered his secret."

"So often the way," Ruth said, sitting next to him, "the secrets coming out after death."

The Tiger and the Coronet

"What was his secret?" Flo asked.

Robert gave a thin smile. "He'd always said he'd had no family, that he had been an orphan from birth with no knowledge of his past. I had no reason to doubt him, or even question it at all. After all, it was all I'd known. Then I found the letters."

"Letters?"

"From a man who was clearly my father's brother. He'd written a number of them many years ago, to addresses I'd never heard of. I suppose my father moved and broke off all ties eventually."

"Do you know what came between them?" Flo asked.

"Only what I could gather from the letters, which isn't very much, I'm afraid. All I know is they mentioned a girl there had clearly been a dispute over. I remember the line 'You can't keep her hidden from me'. I had wondered if she was my mother at first, but it was clear they were talking about someone much younger."

"You didn't know your mother?" Flo asked.

"Not really. She died from a brief illness when I was four. My father never remarried and raised me alone."

"What did you do after finding the letters? Did you try to contact your uncle?"

"I did, and it wasn't difficult. He was still at the same address given in the letters. I wrote to him and informed him of his brother's death. He wrote back with a single line, asking if I had my father's papers in my possession and that he would like to see them. I was a bit put out. I'd asked if we could meet, so I could understand the family more. I told him that my father had left very little in the way of papers. He wasn't one for clutter. If he had no use of something, he threw it out. Then I reiterated my desire to meet with him."

"And what was his reply?"

"He asked me to send everything I had to him at once. Of course I refused. Eventually, he said to bring everything I had to him as soon as I could. It was hard for me to get away with work and everything, but we eventually arranged a date. Unfortunately, he passed away before we could meet."

Flo frowned. "And yet he left you some inheritance?"

"Not to me exactly, nor to my father, really. He left no will at all."

"No will?"

"Nothing at all. I rather got it by default. The family's law firm was aware of my father having handled the family's affairs for many years."

"So you inherited everything?"

"All of it," Robert said in a weak voice, as though he still couldn't quite believe it himself.

"Not an insignificant amount as well, I gather," Ruth said with a smile.

Robert smiled as his cheeks reddened.

"And what has all this got to do with Charles Becker?" Flo asked.

Robert sighed. "It seems he lived near my uncle and knew him very well."

Chapter Twenty

"So the will left everything to the nephew?" Jessie asked.

"That's right," Charles said bitterly, "and the nephew in question is that bespectacled imbecile, Robert Pearce."

Jessie blinked a few times and then frowned.

"I'm sorry, but I'm not sure I understand why you're so angry at him? Shouldn't he inherit from his family, even if they were estranged? What's your connection to the family?"

Charles gave a single, bitter cough of laughter. "My father fell from a horse and died when I was eight years old. We'd been a household on the rise. My father was making quite the name for himself in the city, and money had never been an issue. Then, with my father's passing, it was. We didn't really know Victor at that time. His estate lived a few miles from the village where we lived, and of course, everyone knew of him. He employed half the people in a twenty-mile radius."

He took a deep breath and leaned forward, placing his elbows on his knees, his eyes scouring the floor.

"He had heard of my father's accident and visited the house to give his sympathy. The moment he looked at me and I saw his eyes, full of sympathy and pity, I became angry. I shouted at him, told him he had no right to mourn a man he hadn't known. I told him to get out of our house and never come back, but he did. After that, he came back once a week, without fail. After a time I became less angry, we began to talk. Not about my father, but about all sorts of things. His estate, fishing, sport. His son had died years before and I think I sort of filled that hole in his life."

He paused, and Jessie waited a moment before prompting him to continue further.

"You became close?"

Charles looked up at her, and she saw that his eyes were shining with emotion.

"He became like another father to me, a better father, if I'm totally honest."

"And so," Jessie said, "When he died, you expected to inherit at least something from his estate?"

"Like I said," Charles answered, his jaw tight, "he had never mentioned any other family in all the years I had known him. More than that, he had made it very clear to me that I would be left in charge of his estate when he passed. Then, he asked me to go away for a while."

"Go away?" Jessie asked.

"He said he wanted me to see some of the life of the world before I settled down. He told me to move to London and enjoy myself, and he would give me a monthly stipend for me to spend as I pleased."

"And that's what you did?"

The Tiger and the Coronet

The young man nodded, "Until I received word that he had been taken ill. I rushed back, but... I was too late."

He ran his hand through his black hair. "After a few days I reached out to his lawyers. I was keen to get the formalities over so I could take stock of how the estate was positioned." He gave a mirthless laugh. "I was told in no uncertain terms that I was not named in Victor's will. I didn't believe it and demanded to know who was included, he wouldn't tell me, of course. It was only weeks later when I was back in London that I heard the rumour that it had gone to a previously unknown relation."

"Robert Pearce," Jessie said, nodding.

"Yes, though I didn't know at the time. I only learned that wonderful detail here." He said bitterly, his lips thinned. "The thought of that weak fool taking over Victor's estate makes my blood boil."

Chapter Twenty-One

"Did you manage to calm him down?" Flo asked.

"I'm not sure if he's actually calm as such, but I don't think he's going to try to start a fight," Jessie replied.

They were back in Flo's room, looking through the window at the expanse of lawn for signs of the tiger, Duchess. They had left the two men they had been talking to with a second drink and met in the hallway before coming back up the stairs for some privacy.

"Anyway," Jessie continued, "Let's focus on the real matter at hand. What do you think of the butler, Jenkins?"

"I'd wager that Charles Becker didn't offer him a glass of port out of the kindness of his heart," she said with eyebrows raised.

"You think he drugged him?" Jessie nodded.

"Don't you?" Flo asked.

"I do," Jessie replied with a smile. "That's why I asked him."

"You asked him?!" Flo asked, incredulous. "Don't you think that was a little dangerous?!"

"I didn't ask him outright," Jessie said with a smile. "I just said that I'd heard he'd shared some sort of fine port with Jenkins."

"And what did he say?"

Jessie laughed. "He could barely remember it at first. Apparently, he, and most of the others, had been drinking heavily since lunch that day. He said he'd found the port, which apparently was quite a fine vintage, and had been indulging when he bumped into Jenkins in the library and spilt some of his drink on him. It sounds like Charles is a happy drunk as, once Jenkins had cleaned himself up, he insisted on him having a drink to make up for the incident."

"Having met Jenkins, I'm surprised he agreed. He seems a stickler for the rules of his position."

"I assume he has a weakness for port," Jessie laughed. "The mood he was in, I wasn't going to start accusing him of drugging someone. That said, it must have been him. He would have wanted Jenkins out of the way so that he and Beth could take the coronet more easily."

"If they'd been drinking, it might have made them bold enough to do it," Flo agreed, "or stupid enough."

"And with missing out on getting the inheritance he thought was rightfully his, he has a motivation for obtaining money."

"Can you really see him stealing the coronet, though? Or anyone, for that matter. How on earth could you hope to sell it without being discovered?"

"There's always someone willing to buy something like that, even if it's only to shut it away and never let anyone see it again."

"Really?" Flo said, amazed, "You think there are people who would buy it just to stare at it themselves, but keep it hidden, a secret, forever?"

"I know there are," Jessie said, turning to the window again.

Flo noticed her voice was different as she said this, almost a tone of resignation.

"There are people who do things just for the thrill of knowing they can. Knowing they can get away with it."

Flo studied her friend's profile thoughtfully. It sounded as though she was talking from experience, and from a pained experience at that.

"Anyway," Jessie said, "We're missing the obvious."

"Which is?"

"We both believe Charles Becker, possibly working with Beth, drugged the butler to get him out of the way so they could steal the coronet."

"Maybe," Flo said, tilting her head left and right uncertainly.

"And you suggested before that, when we saw Hector's body, there were no defensive wounds."

Flo frowned, then her eyes widened. "You mean Hector may well have been drugged as well?"

"It would make sense, wouldn't it?" Jessie said, one eyebrow arched.

Flo gasped as her hand moved to her mouth involuntarily.

"What is it?" Jessie asked, her grey eyes alight with excitement.

"Something Evans, the housekeeper, said when we were talking to the butler. She mentioned 'missing pills' I was about to ask her what she meant when all this business between Charles and Robert started."

"Missing pills," Jessie repeated thoughtfully.

"And then there's this," Flo said, moving across to the dressing table and lifting the lid on a small jewellery box.

The Tiger and the Coronet

She turned, holding a small ball of cotton wool in her hand. "I found this on the path by the menagerie. Don't you think it could have come from a pill bottle?"

Jessie nodded and folded her arms. "Ok, let's start by going through what we know about Friday night. The maid saw Charles and Beth heading towards The Gilt room."

"She says she did," Flo corrected.

"You think she's lying?"

"I think we should assume everyone is until we have some proof."

"Ok," Jessie said, putting her hands up to show she conceded the point. "The maid said she saw them going to The Gilt room."

"And Robert Pearce said he saw them going towards the menagerie from his bedroom window the same night," Flo added.

'Right," Jessie said, clicking her fingers.

"We've missed a step though," Flo continued. "Jenkins."

"Yes!" Jessie said enthusiastically. "We know Charles gave the butler a drink of port and soon after, he felt ill and went to bed. Getting him neatly out of the way for whatever they were planning to do with the coronet."

"And it makes sense they would try the same trick with Hector," Flo continued. "He lived in a room at the menagerie, so they would have known that he might spot them with the coronet, but..." Flo frowned.

"What is it?" Jessie asked.

"Why would they have been going to the menagerie in the first place?"

Jessie frowned now, too. "Maybe to hide the coronet to get it later?"

"No," Flo said, shaking her head. "Why would they

choose to hide the thing where they know someone is staying? There are all manner of hiding spots around without a person able to spot them. They could have shoved it in a bush or something."

They stared out of the window for a moment before Jessie spoke again.

"Maybe Robert Pearce was lying."

"About seeing them head towards the menagerie? But it all fits. They drugged the butler, and someone drugged Hector." Flo sighed. "We need to speak to Evans again. I want to know what she meant about these missing pills."

"Ok, we'll put that top of the list. What about this telegram of Mary's?"

Flo once again moved to the jewellery box and pulled out the telegram that she had seen Mary Preston throw on the fire and read it aloud again.

"Take action now, stop. Reward is waiting. Stop. Just need to grasp it, stop."

"What on earth do you think that's all about?"

"Well," Flo answered, "the obvious answer is there's some sort of financial trouble and her 'taking action' is about stealing the coronet."

Flo nodded, "We need to ask Rathbone about her family, her personal situation, etc. There may be something there that points to motive.

"Ok, what about the others?" Jessie said. "Robert, Ruth and Thadd."

"I can't see any motive for Robert to steal the crown. He's just come into a significant sum of money."

"I agree, Ruth and Thadd?"

"The only motivations I can see for them are political ones," Flo said thoughtfully.

"You're going to have to explain that to me," Jessie

answered. "what motivation would they have for stealing the coronet?"

"These are difficult times for the country. The problems in Ireland have stirred up similar feelings in Scotland and Wales. I'd imagine the whole point of passing the coronet back to the people of Wales is to reenforce good will."

"And you think Ruth and Thadd, being Welsh, might have sympathies with the Irish?"

"Well, we know Thadd has political ambitions. He's in the only Welsh ministerial office I've ever heard of."

"And Ruth?"

"When we first met everyone on the terrace, she made a comment to Thadd, implying he was some sort of a puppy on the leash of the British Empire."

"Interesting," said Jessie thoughtfully, "but it's a bit thin, isn't it?"

"It is," Flo sighed, "come on, let's go and find the housekeeper."

Chapter Twenty-Two

"Pills?" Evans said, confused before her small, round eyes widened in recognition. "Oh, of course, Miss Robbins' sleeping pills."

"Miss Robbins?" Flo asked.

"That's right. Miss Robbins said she had sleeping pills on her nightstand and says they just vanished." The woman lifted her chin, pulling her body straight to her full, though still short, height. "I told her, none of my girls would ever take something from a guest's room and I'd swear on it. She must have mislaid them herself or something."

"When was this? When did the pills go missing?"

Evans blinked, as though confused by the question. "Well, it was the Thursday."

"The day before the coronet was taken," Flo said to Jessie.

"I don't see what some mislaid pills have to do with the coronet," Evans said before seeming to check herself, realising she was talking to guests and not scullery maids. "Sorry ma'am," she said, bowing her head slightly, "I didn't mean to speak out of turn."

"Oh, nonsense," Jessie said dismissively. "the question is, which of the guests were here when they went missing?"

Evans wrinkled her pug nose in thought, "Well, all of them were here by then."

Flo sighed. "So any of them could have gone into Ruth's room and taken them."

"But why would anyone do that, Miss?" Evans asked.

Jessie and Flo exchanged a look, unsure of how much to reveal about their thinking. It was Jessie that decided for them.

"Evans, you know Mr Rathbone brought here us to find the coronet?"

"Yes, Miss," Evans nodded, her small eyes alight with excitement.

"Well, we could use your help if you're willing to offer it?"

"Oh yes, Miss, of course!" She answered hurriedly.

"Great! Then what we need from you is to get everyone on the staff to keep their ear out."

Evans's animated expression faltered slightly.

"Oh, I realise this might go against your professional sensibilities," Jessie jumped in quickly, "but Mr Rathbone has given us scope to do whatever it takes, given the serious circumstances."

"Oh, of course, Miss," Evans said, looking relieved.

"So, talk to everyone on the staff. Ask them to listen out for everything they can hear from the guests."

"About the coronet, miss?" Evans asked.

"No," Jessie said, "about anything. Get them to feed it all back to you and if you think there's anything that sounds like it's the right stuff, you come and let us know."

"Oh, I will miss, I will."

After a few more reassurances, Evans left them, and they turned back to the window.

"Do you think that was a wise move?" Flo asked.

"Of course," Jessie laughed, "no one hears gossip like the staff, no matter how much they claim to professionalism. We need to know what's going on here. We're running out of time and now with Hector's death..."

Flo nodded. "It's connected, I'm sure of it. We just need to work out how or why."

"One thing's for sure, Charles Becker and Beth Armstrong know something about it."

"Beth is the weak link in the chain. We need to talk to her alone."

Jessie smiled wolfishly. "I think I can arrange that."

Chapter Twenty-Three

Flo had to admit she was in equal parts impressed and jealous with the ease that Jessie approached her task. She had stalked her prey, Charles, across the ground floor of the house and found him and Beth in the billiards room where he was playing Thadd.

"Ladies," Thadd said with a slight nod of his head, "Do either of you play?"

"I've probably played more games of eight-ball than you've had hot dinners," Jessie said in a light tone as she moved around the table towards Charles, who stood watching as Thadd bent to take a shot. She reached out and took the cue from him. "And what about you Charles, would you say you're an expert player?"

Flo's eyes widened as she watched her friend run her hand up and down the cue in a way that was so suggestive she felt her own cheeks flushing from the other side of the room.

Next to her, Beth Armstrong jumped from the sofa she had been sitting on and stared across the room with nostrils flared and arms folded.

"Why don't you let me take your next shot," Jessie said softly as one hand gently touched Charles' chest before she turned to the table.

Flo could see the effect on Charles was considerable. His mouth formed a small 'O' and his eyes had the look of a rabbit in headlights.

"Charles," Beth said in a sharp tone, "I'm feeling awfully cooped up here, I'd like you to take me for a walk around the house,"

Charles didn't even look up, let alone answer. His eyes were bulging as Jessie bent down in front of him to take her shot. One that she seemed to be taking some time over, in Flo's opinion. Not only that, she seemed to be having some difficulty in positioning herself for the shot, at least her the wriggling of her hips was suggesting so. Flo noticed a light sheen of sweat developing on Charles's forehead.

"Charles!' Beth snapped, finally making him look up, but only for a second.

"Not now, Beth," he said in a faraway voice as his gaze returned to the action at the pool table.

Beth gave a sudden cry of frustrated anguish and headed for the door.

Jessie made the shot she was attempting, stood up, winked at Flo and gestured with her head towards the door. Flo nodded back and followed Beth into the hallway.

"Are you ok Beth?" Flo called after the slim figure hurrying across the hallway.

Beth paused and turned her head and gave a cold, "I'm fine thank you," before turning again and heading into the library.

Flo waited a few moments before taking a deep breath and heading in after her. The young woman stood looking away from Flo with her hands on the back of a leather armchair, her shoulders shook slightly.

"Can I get you a drink?" Flo said softly.

She saw Beth's back tense, then relax. She turned, wiping her eyes, and nodded. "I'm sorry," she said as Flo moved to the drinks cabinet in the room. "I'm being silly, I know."

"Oh, I don't think so," Flo said in what she hoped was a sympathetic tone, despite not really knowing what Beth was talking about.

"I feel like some silly lovesick schoolgirl, following Charles around like a puppy all the time."

"Oh, I don't think anyone thinks that," Flo said automatically.

"Of course they do," Beth replied testily. "it's true after all." She took the drink Flo offered her and sighed. "I just wish the damn fool would notice me."

"Oh come now, the two of you seem inseparable."

"Oh yes, we're the best of chums alright," Beth muttered, swirling her drink and staring at it as though her gaze could burn a hole through the bottom of the glass, "but that's all it is for Charles. I'm just someone to drag along on his little stunts."

"Is that what happened on Friday night?" Flo said.

Beth looked up at her sharply. "I don't know what you mean."

"We know the two of you took the coronet," Flo replied. "You were seen with it heading out towards the menagerie."

Beth stared at her for a moment before the defiant look on her face broke and she shook her head. "Damn stupid thing to do," she said with a sigh. "Another stupid idea of Charles's that I went along with, like some love-sick fool."

"Where is it?" Flo said, trying to keep the excitement out of her voice.

The guarded look immediately returned to Beth's eyes. "I've no idea,"

"Oh come now Beth, there's no reason to keep the thing a secret. The jokes worn rather thin by now, hasn't it?"

"It's not that, I..." she tailed off and, looking down at her handsand began turning a ring on her right hand.

"Poor Hugo is going crazy with worry," Flo said. "If you just tell us where the coronet is, we can all relax. Well, apart from the tiger confining us to the house!" She said with a laugh. One that faltered as she realised Beth hadn't joined her.

"That's just the problem," Beth said in a voice so thick with a sudden emotion that it made Flo blink in surprise as she watched tears form in the young woman's eyes.

"Beth, what is it?"

Beth pulled a handkerchief from a pocket and dabbed at her eyes. "Poor Hector!" She said before blowing her nose, "I just know it was our fault, no matter what Charles says."

Flo's heart was now thumping in her chest.

"What do you mean, Beth?" She asked, her voice sounding flat and cold to her own ear, "how can you and Charles taking the coronet as a prank have possibly ended up with Hector's death?"

Beth seemed to gather herself as she looked up and met Flo's eyes. "We threw the damned thing into the tiger's cage," she said in a sudden rush.

Flo stared at her in incomprehension. "Into the cage?"

"Yes! Why don't you see? That's how poor Hector..." she broke off again, this time into altogether more dramatic sobs.

Flo muttered an exclamation under her breath as she put together Beth's train of thought.

"You think Hector went into the enclosure to fetch the coronet?"

"Of course he did!" Beth shouted in frustration. "We got him killed as surely as if we'd mauled him ourselves!"

Flo was searching for words of comfort when something occurred to her.

"When you threw the coronet in the cage, did you see where it landed?"

"Of course," Beth said as she regained her composure again, "it landed on its side and rolled and stayed leaning up against the back wall. It would have been clear as day for anyone stood outside the cage."

"Let alone for someone stood inside it," Flo said quietly.

"I beg your pardon?"

"Oh, it's nothing. Ignore me. Are you sure the coronet would have been clear for anyone to see?"

"Absolutely. That's why Hector got himself killed. He must have seen it and thought he could take it for himself."

"Or recover it for Hugo," Flo said.

"Oh, I hadn't thought of that," Beth said, looking even more dejected.

"Is there any way Charles could have recovered the coronet afterwards somehow?"

"Without getting eaten by that horrible beast that's now prowling the grounds? Not a chance. I'm telling you, Flo, Charles and I don't have the thing. It must still be in the cage."

Chapter Twenty-Four

"Flo, darling!" Hugo exclaimed as she came back into the hallway, "I have fantastic news!"

"Oh?" Flo said, hoping to hear that the coronet had been found.

"The animal handler will be here in a few hours to handle sedating Duchess."

"Oh, that's great news," Flo said, a little disappointed.

"It's such a relief to know that she'll be returned to her enclosure safe and sound," Hugo beamed before his smile faltered, "Then we can deal with the Hector situation as well, of course."

Although the words he had used sounded flippant, Flo could see the genuine pain on his face. She suspected he was unused to talking about such things.

"Any news on the coronet by any chance?" He asked hopefully.

"I'm afraid not," Flo answered, "but I think we're narrowing down the possibilities. Excuse me, I need to talk to Jessie. Ah, here she is!"

The Tiger and the Coronet

Jessie emerged into the hall from the billiard room with a wide grin.

"How did it go?" She asked before Flo could speak.

"Not quite in the direction I expected."

"What do you mean?"

"Well," Flo began, "Charles and Beth did take the coronet."

Hugo gasped and took a step backwards as though dealt a physical blow. "And after I welcomed them into my home!"

"So they have it stashed away somewhere?" Jessie asked.

"No, that's just it. I don't think they know where it is. At least Beth doesn't."

Jessie frowned and folded her arms. "You're going to have to explain that."

"They took the coronet as a joke and threw it into the tiger's cage."

"In with Duchess?!" Hugo exclaimed.

"Wait a minute," Jessie said, looking at Flo.

"You're thinking the same as me, aren't you?"

"What? What are you thinking?" Hugo asked, desperately trying to keep up with the conversation.

"When we discovered what had happened to Hector, we had to hide from the tiger in the cage," Flo said, turning to him.

"Oh dear, I'm terribly sorry," he stammered.

"The point is," Flo continued, "we were in that cage and there was no sign of the coronet."

"It could have landed out of sight somewhere," Jessie mused.

"I don't think so," Flo replied. "Beth said it landed

upright against the back wall in plain sight. Anyone would have spotted it there."

"But that doesn't make sense," Jessie said. "We would have seen it, surely?"

"Unless someone else had taken it from the cage after they'd left it there," Flo said.

It was Jessie's turn to exclaim in shock, "Hector!"

Flo nodded, "That's why Beth was so upset. She thinks their prank backfired horrifically."

"You mean," Hugo said, his face pale, "That Hector tried to retrieve the coronet from the cage and that's how Duchess," he swallowed, "did what she did?"

"Maybe," Flo said, frowning.

Jessie gave her a quizzical look, but another voice spoke before she could.

"So their silly little prank has cost a man his life."

The three of them turned to see Mary Preston descending the stairs, with Ruth Robbins and Robert Pearce in tow. As she reached the hallway, she moved to Hugo and took his hand in hers.

"And poor Duchess is the one who has had to suffer," she said, patting Hugo's hand with a sympathetic expression.

"I'm sure no one is to blame," Robert Pearce said, his high voice sounding even more uneasy than it usually did.

"And the coronet is presumably still with poor Hector out there somewhere," Ruth said, shaking her head sadly.

"Yes," Flo cut in before Jessie could correct her, "the coronet is probably still out there in the tiger's cage now."

Jessie shot her a quick glance, but clearly knew to play along. "Once the animal specialist arrives in a few hours, Duchess can be returned to her cage, and we can retrieve the coronet, ready for the royal visit."

"All neat and squared away, eh?" They turned to the billiard room door where Thadd had just appeared and spoken from, "except for poor Hector, that is."

There was a moment of silence as Thadd walked over to the group in the hallway, Charles behind him. Flo looked around the faces as everyone's thoughts dwelled on Hector.

"A terrible accident," Charles said, breaking the silence, "but I suppose he knew the risks of working with the beast."

"That's rather rich coming from someone who contributed to his death!" Hugo erupted, his face shading crimson, "And I'll warn you to not call Duchess a beast any longer while you are under my roof!"

"Yes," Thadd said, "come on Charles, bad form being so flippant about a man's death."

"Oh, really?" Charles snapped back at him, "Well, I guess you'd know all about 'bad form', wouldn't you, Thadd? You've bet on so many losing horses the jockeys are refusing to ride anything you back!"

"Really," Mary said, her hand still holding Hugo's, "Why do all the male guests in this house seem so determined to abuse Hugo's hospitality?"

"Oh, be quiet Mary!" Beth shouted. "you can butter up to Hugo as much as you want, but we all know it's not going to get you anywhere."

There was another heavy silent pause as various members of the group glared at each other.

"Come on Hugo," Mary said, leading him towards the drawing room. "Let's get you a drink."

Her movement seemed to spur the others into action and people starting drifting away from the hall to various rooms.

"Well," Jessie said when they were alone once more, "I think it's safe to say that everyone's on edge."

"Do you know what?" Flo said, with a slight grin on her face, "We seem to find far more out when people are at each other's throats." She looked at Jessie and raised one eyebrow.

Jessie grinned wolfishly at her. "Are you suggesting we maybe stir the pot a little?"

"It might be worth a try," Flo answered, feeling a slight thrill of guilt at the idea.

"Flo Hammond," Jessie said in a harsh tone, putting both hands on her hips, "I had no idea you had such a devious side to your personality!"

Flo rolled her eyes. "I think the company I keep might be rubbing off one me. Come on. I know just where to start."

Chapter Twenty-Five

Around half an hour later, the house was gathered for lunch in the dining room. The atmosphere was stilted, to say the least. Grim, hard faces were positioned around the long table, the only exception being Hugo. The host's expression was more one of contrition as he broke the silence.

"I think it's only right that I offer an apology to all of you," he began, "I lost my temper in a most inappropriate way. As your host, I must do better."

"I still say you have nothing to apologise for," Mary said. "Guests should show more respect to their host."

Flo saw Beth's eyes roll in his head, and with it, her opportunity.

"I see you don't agree, Beth?" She said, causing the young woman to stiffen as all eyes turned to her.

"Well, I think I should also apologise as I raised my voice earlier."

"Then perhaps it's Mary's motives you have an issue with?" Flo jumped in before she could continue.

"Well, I..." Beth stammered.

"Yes, please tell us exactly what your issue is, Beth," Mary said, her voice suddenly hard like iron.

Flo saw Beth's jaw clench and her eyes burned more brightly.

"Very well," she said, placing her hands palm down on the white tablecloth in front of her, "I think it's abundantly clear you have arrived at this house with the express intention of snaring Hugo, and no doubt his money."

"How dare you!" Mary said, pushing her chair back with force as she stood, throwing her napkin onto her plate. "May I suggest you stop taking your frustrations about unrequited love out on others, and maybe focus on the idiot who's taking you for a ride?" She turned and strode to the door, only stopping to tell Evans, who hovered in the corner, that she would take her lunch in her room.

"Really, Beth," Charles said, "I do wish you would think before you speak sometimes."

Beth's face turned red as it contorted in anger. "You're a fine one to talk, shouting at poor Robert for no other reason than his uncle respected family!"

"Family?" Charles shouted back, his own rage surfacing quickly. "They were no family to Victor! I was like a son to him, and I know he would have wanted me to inherit."

"Or is it just that you wanted a father figure so desperately you invented most of your relationship with him in your head?" Beth snapped back.

Charles' lips thinned and his face paled with anger, but he said nothing.

Thadd cleared his throat and straightened his back as he spoke. "I think we can all agree that it's been a particularly difficult and stressful couple of days," he said, looking around the table. "The animal specialist will be here soon to deal with Duchess, and the police can access the grounds.

Let's focus on what will be a special occasion in a few days when his majesty arrives."

"Don't you think it's time to drop the holier than though attitude Thadd?" Ruth said, "You've got half the bookies in South Wales after you and it's not exactly a secret that you helped arrange this little visit at Trelawny House in the hope Hugo here would bail you out of your debts in return. In fact," she said, looking around the table herself with a slight smile on her face, "Isn't it time everyone just admitted they are here for reasons of their own rather than any nonsense like national pride?"

"Oh? And what's your reason?" Mary asked, her voice like cut glass.

"Oh, that's easy," Ruth said with a laugh. "I'm here for the status boost. Being here for a royal visit won't do anyone's reputation any harm. Lord knows my family could do with it."

There was a brief period of silence where the guests seemed to focus on filling their plates from the selection of cold meats and cheeses arranged on the long table in front of them. It was Jessie who picked up the conversation again.

"I think it's only fair that Flo and I are completely honest about what we think has happened here," she said, her voice ringing out slightly more loudly than was strictly necessary, bringing all eyes to her. "I know in the hall there was talk that Hector may have entered the cage to retrieve the coronet, and that's what got him killed, but we don't think so." She looked around the faces at the table before settling on Flo, who, keeping her face impassive, gave a small nod for her to continue. "We believe that Hector was drugged and left to die. Someone who retrieved the coronet from the enclosure and let Duchess loose. That someone is sitting at this table, and we intend to find out who it is."

"You can't be serious," Charles said, "Not content with implying we somehow caused his accidental death, you're now saying we deliberately murdered the man?!"

"It was only you and Beth that knew the coronet was in the enclosure," Thadd said in a level tone.

"But why would we throw the bloody thing in there if we wanted to steal it? We could have just run off with it there and then!"

"Maybe you decided you needed some sort of cover," Thadd shrugged.

"Or maybe you saw us that night and decided that taking the coronet could make all your gambling debts vanish?" Charles snapped back. "How long have they given you to pay them back exactly before they start breaking bones?" Or maybe we should look at the person around this table I already suspect of being underhanded when it comes to money and greed." He turned and looked straight at Robert Pearce, who blinked back at him in shock.

"I'm afraid I must insist on repeating that I never met my uncle and certainly didn't force him to ensure I received his estate."

"Oh, of course he did," Charles said in a tone dripping with sarcasm, "It wouldn't surprise me in the least if you took the coronet in order just to return it later to play the big hero. We all know what you're lacking here, and after swindling me out of my rightful inheritance, it's not money."

"And what is it, then?" Ruth asked.

"Isn't it obvious?" Charles said, staring at Robert with a malevolent grin, "He's a nobody! He's a jumped up bean counter who's planning on playing lord of the manor. He probably thinks being the hero in something like this would get him accepted by high society." He gave a derisive laugh and filled his wine glass liberally.

"Wait a minute," Thadd said. "You said Hector was drugged. Who on earth would drug him and how? Why would anyone even want to kill him?"

"I think the 'why' is fairly obvious," Charles said, gesturing at Flo and Jessie. "These two lunatics think I wanted him dead because he saw me take the coronet."

"I think Ruth can explain the where the drugs come in," Jessie said, cutting off what Flo thought was an incoming rant from Charles who had already refilled his glass again.

"Me?" Ruth said in surprise, before her pale blue eyes suddenly widened as her hand went to her mouth, "Oh! You mean my pills!"

"What pills?" Hugo asked.

"I had some sleeping pills taken from my room," Ruth answered."I assumed a maid had taken them."

"And you think those were used to drug poor Hector?" Hugo asked, his voice strained.

"Yes," Jessie answered firmly. "We think he was given the pills to get him out of the way," she turned to Charles. "I wonder if the person tested out the pills beforehand."

Charles frowned at her. "What on earth do you mean by that?"

"It was funny how the butler, Jenkins, was taken ill after you shared a glass of port with him, wasn't it?"

Charles's mouth opened and then closed again.

"My god Charles," Beth exclaimed in a breathy voice, "What have you done?"

"For god's sake Beth!" Charles barked back as he rose from the table. "You can't believe any of this nonsense? You were with me when we threw the coronet in that bloody tiger's enclosure!"

"Maybe I saw exactly what you wanted me to see? Maybe you used me as a convenient witness?" Beth snapped back. "It wouldn't exactly be the first time you've manipulated me for your own amusement, would it?"

Charles threw his hands in the air as he spun away from the table. "Has this whole household lost its mind?!"

"This household," Jessie said firmly, "has not lost its mind. It has, though, lost two things. A coronet, and more importantly, a human life."

"For goodness' sake, the thing is just going to be lying on the ground out there in the menagerie somewhere." Charles muttered angrily as he ran his hands through his dark hair, "no doubt dropped by Hector when he was trying to steal it and the tiger attacked him."

"We know that's not what happened," Jessie said.

"You know nothing!" Charles shouted, turning to her before his eyes scanned those still sat around the table. "Can't you see what's happened here? Beth and I pulled a harmless prank. Unfortunately it appears that greed then got the better of poor Hector and he paid the price for it. That's it, that's everything. There's no mystery here, nothing that hasn't been created in the minds of these two charlatans in any case." He turned to Hugo at the head of the table, "I'm sure you had good intentions in inviting these women to the house, and I'm sorry if what we did in jest has caused you any discomfort, but I urge you to see common sense and not get caught up in what these women are trying to stir up in order to no doubt sell another story to the press for their own financial gain."

He turned to glare at Beth with his hands on his hips, and she met his eye with an equal ferocity before suddenly standing up and leaving the room. With one more glance around the seated guests, Charles followed her.

"What do you plan to do now" Thadd said, looking between Jessie and Flo. Flo looked up at his pale face and saw that all pretence at being the commanding figure of modern politics had left him. He looked as shocked at recent events at anyone around the table.

"I really don't think there's anything we can do until Duchess is dealt with and the police can come in and investigate," Flo said, annoyed with this reality even as she spoke it. "I would say, though, if there's anything that any of you know about the events here that you haven't yet shared, now would be the time to do so."

There was an awkward silence as everybody in the room seemed to find something of interest to stare at on the table in remnants of the breakfast in front of them.

"I have to say," Ruth said. Eventually, I don't fancy the idea of just waiting here in the house with a murderer."

This caused everyone to look up, all with furrowed brows, as though in concerned agreement.

"Especially," Ruth continued, turning to Robert's round face next to her as she placed her hand on his on the table, "if he could mean harm to Robert."

Robert gave a nervous, high laugh before reaching with his left hand to pat Ruth's.

"Oh, I'm sure we're all just getting carried away," he said, though his voice and manner did not quite match this sentiment. He reached for the half-drunk cup of tea in front of him and Flo noticed it shake slightly as he put it to his lips and drank before speaking again "I'm sure whatever happened with Hector was some tragic accident, and even if it weren't, I can't imagine our little understanding earlier would result in him doing anything rash."

"A little misunderstanding?" Ruth said, "he thinks you've stolen his rightful inheritance!"

"I have to say," Thadd chimed in, "That does sound like a good motive for a murderer, and he did seem very angry earlier."

"You know Thadd old chap," Hugo said in a sheepish tone, "I have been wondering if you were maybe the cause of the unfortunate incident with Hector."

"Me?!" Thadd said incredulously, "What on earth are you talking about, man?"

Hugo looked at him and raised one eyebrow, causing Thadd's ferocity to wilt somewhat.

"Sorry, old boy, but I mean to say! Whatever reason do you have to say such a thing?"

Hugo pulled a silver cigarette case from his jacket and lit one before continuing.

"You've got to admit, those thugs that called here the other day were such a frightful lot, the flowers in the hall wilted."

"I've already apologised about that," Thadd said, chastened.

"I know, I know," Hugo said, waving his cigarette dismissively. "All forgiven and all that. What I mean is, what if they came back? What if they'd still been lurking around the grounds? Maybe Hector discovered them and things all got a bit nasty?"

"But Hector was drugged," Ruth said, looking across at Jessie and Flo, "That's what you said, wasn't it?"

"That's what we think at the moment, yes," Flo replied, "But that's just based on what we saw, circumstantial at best."

"Hugo," Jessie said, sitting up in her chair and resting her elbows on the table, "I realise everyone here is your guest, and this is your home, but I really think it's time we conducted a proper search of the house. Including guest bedrooms."

Hugo shook his head as he tapped some ash off his cigarette into the small silver ashtray in front of him. "It's really not the done thing you know," he said wearily, "but if everyone agrees," he shrugged without looking up.

"Does anyone have any objections?" Flo said

"Not me," Ruth said, and there was a chorus of murmurs in agreement.

"Let's give everyone half an hour to cool off and then we'll start," Jessie said.

Chapter Twenty-Six

Flo and Jessie sat in Flo's room, with a stiff gin and tonic each, as they discussed the rather dramatic lunch they had just witnessed.

"Well, I think we definitely ruffled some feathers," Jessie said, "but I wasn't expecting them to all blow up quite so much."

"Do you think we'll find anything when we search?" Flo said.

"Well, the coronet must either be in the house or on the grounds. No one's had much of a chance to get it anywhere else."

"We need to be methodical," Flo said. "Start from the top of the house and work downwards, room by room."

"And we need to make sure everyone is in the same place when we do."

"What do you mean?"

"I doubt someone has the thing in their room. That would be too obvious. If they have stashed it in the house, they might try to move it, so we miss it. Let's say we're about to search the library and that's where it is. All they need to do is take it from there and hide it in a room we've already searched while we're looking in the drawing room or wherever."

"I see your point," Flo said thoughtfully.

She was just about to ask what Jessie thought the best room to keep everyone in was when they heard the scream.

The two women jumped up from their seats, their drinking glasses falling to the floor, and sprinted for the door.

Ruth Robbins was staggering backwards, her face white with shock as she pointed into an open doorway. As they hurried along the corridor, Charles Becker stepped out of the room Ruth pointed at, his right hand and shirt sleeve soaked red with blood.

Others were emerging from their rooms now. Ruth continued to back away from Charles as he stood, looking down at his hands in a daze.

Jessie and Flo moved to the door of the room and looked in. Lying on the floor, a dark bloom of blood spreading from his head, was Robert Pearce.

"My god," Flo said, turning away quickly.

"Charles?" Jessie said, turning away herself and looking at him.

He seemed to snap out of wherever his mind had gone, blinking before replying, "I just found him like that," in a hoarse voice. "I checked if there was a pulse, didn't know what else to do." His right hand came up to run through his hair and then stopped in front of his face as he stared at the blood on it.

"What on earth has happened?" Thadd said as stared between Charles, Jessie and Flo.

Ruth was now being comforted by Hugo, with Mary stood, for once awkwardly, next to them.

Beth, who had arrived last, was staring at Charles with wide eyes.

"Robert's been killed," Jessie said, as she pulled the door of the room, the body lay closed behind her.

The gathering reacted in gasps and cries until Beth moved to Charles, her eyes full of tears.

"Oh, Charles, what have you done?"

"I, I found him," Charles stuttered.

Beth put her arms around his neck and pulled him close.

"I think I better get Ruth some brandy," Hugo said, indicating with a nod of his head the woman sobbing on his shoulder. He turned her away and headed for the stairs, with Mary following.

"Perhaps you should go to your room and get cleaned up," Jessie said to Charles.

Beth pulled away from their embrace and looked at her. "That is Charles's room," she said, pointing to the now closed door. "I'll take him to mine.

She took his arm and led him away from them as Flo and Jessie exchanged glances.

"Has Charles killed him?" Thadd asked, his eyes darting between the door and them.

"We don't know yet, but the police will be here soon and they'll be able to deal with it," Jessie said. "Maybe you should go with Charles and Beth, make sure she's not a lone with him."

Thadd's eyes widened before a determined look came across his face. "Right, will do."

They watched head down the corridor and knock on Charles's room before they turned back to the door next to them.

"We should leave it for the police to see what they can

The Tiger and the Coronet

get from it," Flo said, "but I don't suppose having another look from the doorway would do any harm."

Jessie looked at her with a mixture of surprise and admiration. "I think you're absolutely right," she said as they both moved towards the door of the room and opened it slowly.

"I think it's pretty clear what was used to kill him," Flo said, pointing at a bloodied fire poker which lay next to the body.

She scanned the rest of the room and stopped as the dull gleam of something caught her eye.

"The coronet!" She exclaimed, pointing at the circular gold crown which lay on the floor a few feet behind Robert Pearce's body.

"So, has it been here in Charles's room all along?" Jessie said.

"Unless Robert brought it here?" Flo replied. "But then, why was Robert even in Charles's room?"

"Who do you think is most likely to be able to pull themselves together and talk first, Ruth or Charles?" Jessie asked.

"I think we should talk to Charles. I think the less time he has to concoct a story, the better. We can get something out of him right now that might be useful to the police when they can get here."

Jessie agreed, and they set off down the corridor to where Thadd was standing on guard in the doorway of another room. Inside, Charles sat on a bed with Beth's arm around him. His face was still pale, but his hands were now clean and his eyes looked more alert than they had been.

"How are we doing in here?" Jessie asked as moved into the room behind Thadd.

"How do you think we're bloody doing?" Charles

muttered darkly, "this place is a bloody mad house. I wish I'd never agreed to come."

"Let's start at the beginning," Flo said. "Why was Robert in your room?"

"How the hell should I know?!" Charles barked back. "I was talking to Beth here, in her room. When I headed back to mine, I walked in and found him there on the floor."

"He was already on the floor dead when you got there?"

"Yes, damn it!"

"The coronet is I your room as well," Jessie said.

Charles frowned. "What do you mean?"

"It's on the floor, a few feet beyond the body."

His mouth opened and closed for a moment before he answered, "Robert must have brought it with him. Maybe that's why whoever did this killed him?"

"For the coronet?" Flo said. "If that was the case, why didn't they then take it with them?"

"They must have panicked. Maybe I disturbed them."

"And did you see anyone leave your room, in the corridor outside?"

Charles sighed as he looked at his hands. "No."

"In any case, why would Robert have the coronet?" Jessie said. "It was you and Beth that took it in the first place."

"We've already told you," Beth said, "we left it in the tiger cage and haven't seen it since."

"I'm not sure the police are going to be convinced of that when they get here," Flo said.

Chapter Twenty-Seven

"Can you tell us what happened?" Flo said softly.

Leaving Charles, Beth and Thadd upstairs, they had sought out Ruth, Hugo and Mary. The welsh woman was seated, nursing what looked like a very stiff brandy. Her tears were now gone, but her eyes were still red-rimmed and shining.

"Robert and I were talking in his room. There's been such a lot of funny things going on, with Hector dying and the coronet going missing, and then there's Robert's money,"

Flo and Jessie exchanged a glance.

"Robert's money?" Jessie said. "You mean the five hundred pounds he had with him?"

"Yes," answered Ruth, looking up at her, "It's gone."

"Five hundred pounds?!" Mary exclaimed.

"What do you mean, it's gone?" Flo said, ignoring her.

Ruth blew her nose on a light pink handkerchief before replying. "We'd gone back to our rooms after lunch, like I think most people had. Robert knocked on my door though.

It was only a few minutes later. He said his money was gone. He was in quite a state, as you can imagine."

"And he thought Charles had taken it?" Flo said, her brain only making the connection as the words came from her mouth.

"Yes," Ruth nodded. "With the argument they'd had earlier and with Charles being bitter about Robert's inheritance," she shrugged. "Robert was already sure that Charles had taken the coronet."

"So what did Robert do?" Jessie asked.

"He didn't know what to do. So I said..." She paused as tears filled her eyes. "I said he should go and see Charles about it, but I didn't know he was going right there and then. I thought he'd raise it when the police were here and Charles would see how silly he'd been and would hand the money back."

"So, he then left your room? Did you follow him?"

"No. As I said, I didn't realise he meant to confront Charles there and then."

"But you did leave your room shortly afterwards," Jessie pressed, "and you discovered what had happened?"

"I realised Robert had left his cigarette case in my room. I was going to return it to him, but on my way to his room I passed Charles's and the door was open. When I looked in, I saw Robert on the floor with Charles stood over him." Another fat tear rolled down her pale cheek. "It was so awful."

"Was Charles holding something when you saw him?"

"Holding something?" She frowned. "I don't think so, I... I don't know." She shook her head as though trying to loosen the image from her mind. "Poor Robert. He was such a sweet man."

"You seemed to have become close with him while you were here," Flo said.

Ruth nodded with a smile. "Yes, we seemed to be similar in a way. Both outsiders, both liked animals and nature, both a little odd to tell you the truth," she gave a small laugh. "It's funny, him being invited here was such a huge excitement to him. He was so confused about who he was. He said he wasn't sure if the money he had inherited had been a good or a bad thing."

"Invited here?" Flo said, looking quizzically at Hugo. "Did you invite him?"

"No, I told you," he answered. "Didn't know the chap before I got a letter from him saying that he would be delighted if I would have him stay for a few days and that he was sure his relations knew me or some such thing."

"Do you have the letter now?" Jessie asked.

"Oh no, chucked it weeks ago."

"But Robert definitely told me that he had been invited," Ruth said, looking at Hugo in confusion. "he was particular about it as it had been such a shock for him to receive. What with him not knowing many people."

"I think I may be able to help with that," Mary said, causing all eyes to turn in her direction.

Flo noticed that she seemed to have lost some of her poise. Her face was less of the inscrutable mask than it normally was.

"I'm afraid I haven't been completely honest with you all about my involvement in everything that's happened at Trelawny House." She continued, before turning to Hugo, "I'm afraid I told you that my family was keen for me to come and visit, our two houses being old friends etc, but it wasn't quite true."

"In what way?" Hugo asked.

"Well," Mary said with a small, humourless laugh, "all of it really. The part about me wanting to be an actress is true, and of course, how much my family was against it. That had nothing to do with me coming here, though. The simply fact is I was offered a job."

"A job? You mean an acting job?" Flo asked.

"Yes, exactly. Well, in a way. Firstly, I was told to write some telegrams. I was to invite Robert Pearce and Charles Becker to Trelawny house for the week."

"How did that work?" Jessie asked in confusion. "How could you write and invite them to a place you hadn't even been?"

"It was all arranged by the client. I was given an address for them both and told roughly what to write. Then there was an address to give them for their response, this would be forwarded to a post office in London where I could pick them up. Once they'd agreed, I wrote to Hugo pretending to be them and asking if they could visit."

"So you pretended to be me, and then pretended to be me?!" Hugo said, clearly flabbergasted.

"Yes, I'm afraid so," Mary answered quietly.

Flo couldn't help but be astonished by the change in presence and demeanour of the previously austere woman. Now she seemed smaller, more vulnerable, more human. She realised that Miss Preston was, in fact, a marvellous actress.

"But who organised this? Who was the person that hired you?" Jessie asked.

"I have no idea," Mary said, and for the first time, Mary seemed afraid. "Everything was dealt with through letter. I know that seems odd, but I have to admit, I found it all rather exciting at the time." She gave another small laugh. "I was so desperate to succeed, you see, and although this was certainly strange, the way the letters put it made it seem quite normal. They called it method acting, and that it would be a chance to really test myself." She shook her head sadly.

"What about the telegram you received while you were here?" Flo said.

Mary looked up sharply, first with a confused expression, but it shifted into worry again quickly. "You know about that? I'll admit, that's where I started to panic slightly."

"It said something about you needing to take action, and that a reward was waiting?" Flo pushed.

"I know," Mary answered, "and I couldn't understand it. I'd had instructions to come here, but that was it. I had no idea what on earth that telegram meant or what they expected me to do."

"And they never mentioned taking the coronet at all?" Jessie asked.

"They never mentioned it at all. I didn't even know it was here until I arrived."

"So what was the motivation? What was the point of all this?" Jessie said, throwing her hands up in the air and beginning to pace.

"Someone wanted Charles and Robert both here," Flo said slowly, "So it must be to do with their connection over this inheritance."

"Of course!" Jessie said, snapping her fingers, "someone had an interest in getting the two of them here together this week." She stopped pacing and looked at Flo. "It's Charles, it must be. He wanted revenge for what he saw as an injustice. Maybe he even inherits now?"

"Oh, I'm sure that's not true," Hugo said.

Everyone looked at him, and he squirmed in his seat before glancing at Ruth.

"Oh!" she said, her hand moving to her mouth. "You surely don't think this has anything to do with me?"

"Why would it have anything to do with you?" Jessie asked.

Hugo was still looking at Ruth, concern etched in his expression.

"Oh, it's ok Hugo, you can tell them. I don't mind."

He gave her a small smile and nodded before turning to the others, "It was all a long time ago and much has passed and all that, but when Robert contacted me," he paused and looked up at Mary, "or when Mary did I should say, I realised who it was. We hadn't had contact for a long time, but I knew at once it was Ruth's birth family."

There was a moment of shocked silence before Jessie spoke to Ruth. "Your birth family?"

"I was adopted," Ruth said with a smile. "Mother and Father were always so loving towards me, but I always knew deep down that I was different, even from when I was young."

"The girl that was mentioned in the letters between Robert's father and his brother," Flo said in a rush of sudden understanding.

"Yes," Ruth smiled again. "I couldn't believe that here I was with the opportunity of meeting a half-brother I never knew I had, but also finding out what happened to me, what the circumstances around my adoption were."

"And did you?"

"I'm afraid so. Robert was too discreet to tell you when he mentioned the letters before. We were still working things out, but I think we have a fairly good idea now." She sighed and flattened some imaginary creases in her skirt. "It seems my biological father was something of a brute, particularly where women were concerned. I'm sure my mother wasn't the first of his indiscretions, though I sincerely hope she may have been the last. She was a young parlourmaid in the house, and we believe my father forced himself on her. Previous incidents had been dealt with discreetly, normally using sums of money and a better position elsewhere. This time, however, there was a child."

"You?" Flo said, unable to avoid stating the obvious.

Ruth nodded. "Apparently Robert's father was furious at the family's continued tolerance of his brothers' goings on, and refused to have anything to do with them. He took the parlour maid away from the house with him and never looked back. Unfortunately, my mother died in childbirth. It was decided the best option was to find me a good family where I could grow up away from the knowledge of my past. It was only a year later that Robert's father married himself and he soon came along. His father never spoke of me, or his brother, my father, of course."

"And did Charles know about any of this?" Jessie asked.

"No, I don't think anyone did," Ruth answered, "other than my father, Hugo and me."

"And Thadd, of course," Hugo added.

"Yes, of course," Ruth agreed.

"Thadd knew?" Flo asked.

Ruth smiled softly, "We haven't announced anything yet, but Thadd asked me to marry him last week and I accepted."

Flo and Jessie exchanged a glance.

"We better go and see how Charles is doing," Jessie said, and they both headed for the hallway.

Chapter Twenty-Eight

"Are you thinking what I'm thinking?" Jessie said once they were alone in the hallway.

"Thadd knew that with Robert out of the way. Ruth could be put forward to inherit as his half sister."

"And we know he had gambling debts, proposing to her a week before this gathering seems suspicious timing."

"Miss! Oh miss!" A voice called from the stairs.

They looked up to see the young maid, Jenny, who had descended the first few steps and was now staring down at them with wide eyes.

"Jenny? What is it?" Flo asked.

"It's Miss Armstrong, she's passed out and I can't wake her!"

"Where are Mr Becker and Mr Barnes?"

"They're not there Miss! They were with her when I went past the door a few minutes ago, but they're gone now and she's lying on the floor all in a heap!"

They hurried up the stairs and followed her along the corridor to Beth's room. Inside, the woman lay on the floor at the foot of her bed. As though she had been seated on it and simply slid off. Flo bent down to her and saw that she was breathing normally, if slowly. She lifted one eyelid and saw only the white of her eye.

"I think she's been drugged," she said, standing up.

"Looks like the three of them had drinks," Jessie said, gesturing at a glass which lay on the floor next to Beth and two more which stood on the dressing table.

"So, where have they gone?"

"Excuse me, Miss," Jenny said. I called out when I found Miss Armstrong here and no one replied, so I can't imagine they're upstairs.

"Stay here and make sure she's comfortable, will you, Jenny?" Flo said.

Jenny nodded, and they left the room and headed back for the stairs.

"Do you think they'd have risked going outside?" Jessie asked.

"That's my thinking," Flo answered.

Evans, the housekeeper, appeared as they reached the bottom of the stairs.

"Have you seen Mr Barnes or Mr Becker?" Flo asked her.

"Yes, Miss," the woman answered, her cheeks flushed more crimson than usual, "they just went out of the kitchen door in a right state. Mr Becker looked ever so ill. Mr Barnes was basically holding him up. He said he needed to get him some fresh air, and I said, what about the tiger? and he said they'd be ok and took one of the steaks we were preparing for dinner off the side with him! I thought it was odd, and not altogether good manners, but then the phone rang and..."

"Ok, thank you," Jessie said, both of them already

moving quickly towards the baize door which led back to the kitchens.

"But, Miss," Evans called after them, stopping them short of the door, "it was the police who were calling and they said the large cat expert has arrived and they are moving in to find and tranquillise Duchess." She said, as though repeating verbatim what she had heard on the telephone.

Flo turned to Jessie. "If they're distracted trying to contain Duchess, they may not notice two men trying to leave the grounds."

A look passed between them before they both gave almost imperceptible nods and headed through the door.

Chapter Twenty-Nine

As they passed through the kitchen, they both grabbed large frying pans from the hooks where they hung above the central island with a wordless acknowledgement that, although maybe not a conventional defence against a tiger, it was better than nothing.

They burst from the kitchen door and stood back-to-back, wielding their pans as though they were mighty longswords, but there was no sign of Duchess.

"There," Jessie said after they had taken stock of their surroundings. The expanse of lawn in front of them sloped downwards. To the left, it headed towards the town, and to the right, towards a small copse of trees. It was the latter Jessie was pointing towards.

"What on earth?" Jessie said as she squinted at the figures in the distance.

The more upright of the two was clearly Thadd. He was holding Charles under his arms, dragging him backwards across the grass to the tree line.

"Come on," Flo said, and sprinted away in their direction.

With Thadd encumbered by the clearly unconscious Charles, it wasn't long before they closed the gap. On seeing them, Thadd dropped his burden and faced them, hands on hips.

"He tried to drug Beth and I and then make a run for it," he gestured to Charles.

"You don't look like the one who's drugged to me," Flo said.

"I realised what he was doing and switched my glass with his,"

"And then you decided to drag him out here?"

"No, he was dragging me out here. He only just succumbed to the drug."

"You can't possibly expect us to believe that," Jessie said. "you're dragging him away from the house for goodness sake!"

"Because I was trying to get him away from that," he pointed behind them, and they turned to see the long, powerful form of Duchess loping across the grass towards them. Flo realised with a flush of panic that the beast had been hidden from their view before by the side of the house, now she was moving towards them at a slow, but steady pace.

"Oh my god," Flo said breathlessly.

"The police are here," Jessie said, and Flo looked to her right to see a small group of uniformed officers following a short man dressed in tweeds who held a long rifle, its barrel over his arm.

The next few moments seem to pass almost at once, and yet at the same time, in slow motion.

The group of police, having seen the situation in front of them, were now hurrying across the grass. The short legs of the man with the gun worked furiously beneath him. Flo and Jessie gripped their frying pans more tightly. The tiger advanced.

Suddenly and without warning, the tiger's speed doubled. It's long stride eating up the ground between them so fast that it made Flo gasp in shock. When it was close enough that Flo could see the ripping of its muscular forelegs as it sprang forward, she was pushed aside as Thadd threw himself forward and a deafening crack rang out across the grass.

Flo rolled once before managing to put her hands down and pushing herself up to her knees. Thadd was lying on the ground, his hands at his throat. Duchess lay a few feet away, her hind leg trying to reach, and failing, to scratch at the dart that was jutting from her side. She saw Jessie move towards Thadd and moved to join her.

As soon as she knelt beside him, she saw the blood. It was oozing through his fingers, which were still clasped to his neck. Jessie pulled off the silk scarf she was wearing.

"Move his hands away and we can tie the wound with this," she said authoritatively.

Flo gently pulled Thadd's hands away and almost gagged at the sight of his flesh opening beneath. Jessie quickly applied the scarf and pressed down firmly, causing Thadd's eyes to bulge slightly.

Duchess gave a long, low moan, which Flo felt deep in her stomach. A quick glance was all she needed to confirm that the tiger was going nowhere, though. It had laid on its side now, its tail flicking lazily as its eyes rolled in its head.

A soft, wet noise drew her gaze back to Thadd. He was trying to speak.

"I did it for her," he said in a barely audible whisper.

Jessie shushed him as she stroked his forehead. "Try not to speak, the police are here now."

And they were. The group swarmed round them. Two officers took over from Jessie in attempting to deal with Thadd's injury while one ran to the house to call for a doctor, the small man with the gun attended to the now unconscious Duchess, and Jessie and Flo suddenly found themselves without purpose as they stared at the chaotic scene around them.

Chapter Thirty

Two days after the events of that fateful Sunday at Trelawny House, Flo and Jessie had returned, on the insistence of Hugo, to be present at the symbolic ceremony taking place later that day as the King handed the coronet to the Welsh nation.

The house had a different feel to it than when they had last arrived.

Thadd had not survived his injuries from the tiger. Despite the best efforts of the local police, by the time the doctor had arrived from the town, the young man had died. The three deaths of Hector, Robert and Thadd in such a short period of time had sent the local gossip into a frenzy, but nothing of the incident was reported in the press. The political importance of the King's visit ensured that the media were informed, in no uncertain terms, that the negative publicity of what had occurred at Trelawny House in the days preceding this historic moment were best left out of print.

Hugo was a large part of the mood change at the house. His manner was still light and jovial, but there was a tired weariness to his eyes that showed the weight the last few days had placed on him. This certainly wasn't helped by the fact the menagerie was now scheduled to be closed. The various animals were to be shipped off to zoo's, including Duchess. All except Blue Boy would be gone by the end of the month.

Mary had left, but Charles, Beth and Ruth had stayed on at the house and were now seated in the drawing room along with Hugo, Flo and Jessie.

"I still can't believe it," Hugo said, for what Flo was sure was the twentieth time. "I never would have thought it of Thadd."

"I don't want people to think badly of him," Ruth said. "people in desperate positions are sometimes pushed into desperate acts."

"I'm surprised you can forgive him so easily," Charles said bitterly. "he might have tried to frame me for murder, but he used you more than any of us."

"How so?" Ruth said, looking back at him defiantly.

"Well, it seems his plan was to kill Robert, so that you inherited and then pin it on me. He obviously knew I had a reason for hating Robert, that I considered he had stolen my rightful inheritance. Thadd showed that when he paid Mary to invite both Robert and I here. He'd set it up from the start. For all of this to work, though, he had to persuade you to marry him. This inheritance Robert and I both thought we had rights to was yours, and he wanted that for himself. Don't you think you would have been next to be killed once he had his hands on it?"

Ruth took a moment, as though composing herself, before replying. "Of course, I haven't had time to process everything as yet. I'm sure there are many things to think about regarding the future as well as fully understanding the past few days. One thing I believe, though, is that Thadd cared for me. I believe that to be true, he was genuine in his affection for me. What drove him to do such terrible things can only have been from a terrible desperation, and I hope, a desire to provide us with a comfortable life. No matter how misguided this attempt might have been."

There was an awkward silence as the room considered this a somewhat naïve view.

"If I am to inherit, I will obviously still need someone to run the estate," Ruth continued. "I can't think of anyone better than you, Charles, if you are still interested?"

"I, oh, well," Charles stammered, surprised by the unexpected offer. "I'd be delighted, of course."

"Excellent," Ruth said.

"I think it's high time we heard your theory on what on earth happened here," Hugo said, looking at both Flo and Jessie. "You said on the phone yesterday that you'd put your heads together and come up with something?"

Flo answered. "Yes, but I'm afraid it involves quite a lot of guesswork."

"For those of us without the foggiest clue of what happened," Beth said, "I'm sure it would be appreciated, regardless."

Flo nodded at her. The young woman seemed far more assured and confident since they had last seen her just two days ago. Flo had noted a cool air form her towards Charles, which only seemed to have made him more interested.

"Well," Jessie began with a sigh, "It looks as though Thadd arranged for both Robert and Charles to be here. He wanted them to clash. He hired Mary to arrange this under the pretence of being Hugo. Obviously he couldn't know about the prank Charles and Beth were going to pull with the coronet, but we think he must have got wind of it somehow. Overheard a conversation between them, or maybe even watched them that night. However, he discovered what they were doing, he decided he could use it to his advantage. You'll need to confess something here though, Charles, I think?"

"Confess? What do you mean?" He asked.

"We think it was you that drugged poor Jenkins, the butler," Jessie answered.

"Oh," Charles said, his head dropping slightly. "I'm afraid I did do that, yes. I was sure it was harmless though, just a couple of sleeping pills to make sure he was out of the way for us to get at the coronet."

"My sleeping pills?" Ruth said, "You stole them?"

"What? No!" Charles replied, "Beth had a couple her aunt had given her and we used them."

"We think Thadd knew what you'd done though," Jessie continued, "and that's why he decided to steal Ruth's sleeping pils to use on Hector and Duchess."

"On Duchess?!" Hugo said, looking alarmed.

"Charles and Beth had thrown the coronet into the tiger's cage," Flo said. "No one in their right mind would have just walked in there and got it. They would have had to have sedated Duchess somehow. They probably just threw in some meat they'd added the drug to. Poor Hector was drugged as well. The police have found a bottle of whiskey with a high dose of the sleeping pills in his cabin."

"So once they were both knocked out, Thadd went into the cage and got the coronet. Why leave the cage door open, though?"

"We can't know if it was on purpose or by accident," Flo answered. "he may have just not closed the cage properly in his rush to get out of there. Or, he could have decided that having a tiger on the loose would just add to the confusion and hide what he was trying to do here."

She looked at Ruth, but her expression remained in the faraway, dreamy look it seemed to always have.

"Can I ask," Flo said, turning to Charles, "How did you find out that Robert was the one that inherited the money from Victor Saltern and not you?"

"Ruth happened to mention it to me," Beth said. "I of course, told Charles. Though I wish I hadn't."

"Why do you say that?" Charles asked.

"Because if I'd known what an absolute ass you would make of yourself by shouting at Robert, who was not at fault in any way, I would rather have kept the information to myself."

"It was that clash that Thadd had been waiting for," Jessie said, looking at Ruth. "I assume you had no idea of the significance of this news to Charles when you told Beth?"

"None," Ruth said with a shrug.

"Once Charles and Robert had had their falling out," Jessie continued, "Thadd could put into practice his plan for killing Robert and framing Charles. This would leave Ruth to inherit, and of course, he would then have access to the money once they were married."

"Then why did he drug me and Charles?" Both asked.

"We think he wanted Charles to have the same fate as Hector. He drugged you to keep you quiet, and Charles so he could get him out into the grounds."

"Then why did he protect us in the end?" Charles said. "You said he jumped in front of us all and that's when the tiger got him."

"I don't think we'll ever know," Flo said, turning to look at Ruth. "It certainly would have been perfect for him to have had the person everyone thought was the murderer dead. There would be no chance for Charles to have given another story, to deny that he had killed Robert. It would have ended everything with a nice, neat bow."

"And yet, that isn't what he chose to do," Ruth answered, staring back at Flo just as intently.

"The whole thing is just extraordinary," Hugo said.

"Hadn't we better be leaving soon?" Beth said, looking at the slim watch on her wrist.

"Crikey, yes!" Hugo said, leaping from the sofa. "Come on everyone, the cars will be arriving soon."

They all grabbed coats and hats and ventured outside to the cars, which were already waiting at the foot of the steps to the house.

Jessie, Flo and Hugo entered the first car. Hugo clutching the box that held the coronet as though his life depended on it. Ruth, Charles, and Beth took the other car.

"What was all that about?" Jessie asked Flo as the car began to move away.

"What do you mean?"

"You know perfectly well what I mean," Jessie said. "There seemed to be something passing between you and Ruth, but I have. No idea what."

Flo looked out of the window and sighed. "I'm not sure we'll ever know.

"What does that mean?!" Jessie said, exasperated.

"I'll let you know soon enough," Flo answered, and the tone of her voice made Jessie think that was the end of it.

Chapter Thirty-One

The ceremony itself had been incredibly short and underwhelming as far as Flo had been concerned, they had though, met the king, and that was something you couldn't say every day. Jessie had said that, although he wasn't as tall and imposing as she thought a king ought to be, he did have a penetrating gaze and a twinkle to his eyes that implied a mischievous side, and this she approved of.

When it was all over, drinks were served and the king was whisked off to wherever kings went once their duties were done. It was only a few minutes before Ruth found Flo and they moved without words to the edge of the crowd that gathered on the grass beneath the ancient walls of Cardiff castle.

"It seems," Ruth said once they were far enough away to be able to talk in private, "that you rather think poor Thadd's death was rather convenient for me."

"Wasn't it?" Flo answered. "With his death, I hear the police have dropped their investigations into Hector and Robert's death."

"Of course, why wouldn't they?" Ruth answered breezily.

"It might prevent them from looking at why Thadd committed these crimes more deeply."

"Thadd did what he did for money, to clear his debts," Ruth answered.

"Maybe," Flo said, "Or maybe he did them because he was persuaded to by someone he loved?"

"You flatter me by thinking I could have that much power over a man," Ruth laughed.

"Or maybe his role in all of this was more reduced even than that. Thadd struck me as a passionate, but rather straightforward young man. I don't think he was really cut out for politics at all. Would he really have devised the plan of the fake letters from Hugo to lure Robert and Charles here? Maybe someone else did that."

"You mean me?"

"You're the only person for who all of this has worked out."

"There's no evidence to suggest I knew anything about Thadd's intentions," Ruth said with a smile.

"Do you know what I realised earlier today?"

"What's that?"

"That someone who has planned all of this was an excellent thinker. Not just that though, they were good at improvising, as they did when the coronet was stolen. I suspect Mary actually being invited to the house rather than just be behind the invitations was just another backup to throw suspicion at someone else if needed."

"I'm sure if I was this master criminal you are talking about," Ruth said, "I would be absolutely flattered."

"The thing is, I think that by trying to confuse things as much as they did, they made a mistake."

"Oh?"

"Mary Preston received a telegram while she was at Trelawny house. It was some vague message about taking action and a reward was waiting. All of which, I believe, was meant to make the police think that Mary had something to do with the events of the weekend. Just another false trail to follow, another wave of fog to confuse and obscure. It was a bonus that it could have also related to the theft of the coronet."

"And what of it?" Ruth asked, seeming interested in what Flo was saying for the first time.

"Well, for someone to have sent that telegram, they would have had to have known that Mary would be at Trelawny House. I spoke to Mary, and she swears she told no one at all that she was coming to South Wales, let alone Trelawny."

"She may have let it slip," Ruth said.

"Maybe," Flo conceded, "but I think it is much more likely that the person that sent that telegram was the same person who had set up for Mary to be involved from the beginning. Who orchestrated the invitations to Robert and Charles?"

Ruth said nothing now, but looked back at Flo with interest.

"I wonder if that person took care when sending the telegram to use a post office where they wouldn't be recognised? I'm sire they would have done. After all, I've already said how clever they are. There is a limit, though, to how far this person could have gone to send it. How far would they have travelled, do you think? I wouldn't be surprised if someone was determined enough to check all the post offices within, say, a twenty-five mile radius. They might find one that remembers that telegram and its sender."

"The sending of a telegram would never be enough to convict someone as being involved in the murders," Ruth said flatly.

"No, I think you may be right," Flo said. "However, I do think it might make a wonderful story for my next column, don't you?"

"And if this person were to hear this information, what would you expect them to do with it?" Ruth asked.

"I would expect them to consider they have had a lucky escape, but that their card is marked. They best live an exemplary life going forward. Also, Canada is a good place when looking to start again." Flo looked her in the eye, "Good bye Miss Robbins," and turned, leaving the woman alone with her thoughts.

Afterword

Although this story is entirely fictional, the initial inspiration for it came from a real life character and jewel theft.

If you search online, you will find that Lord Tredegar Evan Morgan really did own a parrot called Blue Boy that swore a lot, He even had a kangaroo which guests could dance with (rather than box).

The event that inspired part of this story was the 1907 theft of the Irish Crown Jewels from Dublin Castle. It remains one of Ireland's most notorious unsolved crimes. Valued at €5m (£4.3m), the jewels, originally crafted from 394 precious stones taken from the English Crown Jewels, were meant for ceremonial use by the Order of St. Patrick.

Typically stored in a bank vault, they were moved in 1903 to a safe in Bedford Tower. However, the safe was too large for the strongroom and was instead placed in the library, doubling as Sir Arthur Vicars' waiting room. Vicars, responsible for their security, was careless with the keys and often showed off the jewels.

On one occasion, while Sir Arthur Vicars was intoxi-

Afterword

cated at a party, Lord Haddo allegedly took his keys, temporarily stole the jewels, and then returned them by post as a prank.

On July 6, 1907, it was discovered that the jewels, along with other valuables, were missing. There was no forced entry, suggesting an inside job. Suspicion fell on Francis Shackleton, brother of explorer Ernest Shackleton, who had access to the keys. Despite investigations by Dublin police and Scotland Yard, no one was convicted.

The theft embarrassed British authorities as King Edward VII had planned to use the jewels during his visit to Ireland. Theories ranged from political motives to personal scandals, but none were proven. To this day, the jewels' fate remains unknown, with speculation they were either broken up or sold secretly

More from AG Barnett

Brock & Poole Mysteries

An Occupied Grave

A Staged Death

When The Party Died

Murder in a Watched Room

The Final Game

―――

The Mary Blake Mysteries

An Invitation to Murder

A Death at Dinner

Lightning Strikes Twice

―――

The Hammond & Circle Mysteries

The Will of the Standing Stones

―――

The Bingham & Gladstone Mysteries

A Rather Inconvenient Corpse

A Bally Awkward Body

―――

SIGN UP AT AGBARNETT.COM TO BE NOTIFIED OF
NEW RELEASES

Printed in Great Britain
by Amazon